Kingdom of Beasts

Byers Publishing LLC
White River Jct, VT 05001

First paperback edition August 2024
Second paperback edition January 2025

Cover Art by Jordan Turk

Library of Congress Control Number TXu002433397

ISBN 9798218564421 (paperback)
ISBN 9798224789160 (ebook)
www.mel-deflorio.com

For Isabel

Trigger warning: This story includes themes of death, loss, grief, and animal cruelty.

TABLE OF CONTENTS

Foreword

Animals watched humans quietly, cautiously, and calmly for centuries. They bore witness to unspeakable horrors not documented in human writing and film. For this reason, they learned to keep their distance from this violent species. It was a simple question of survival.

Long before discovering agriculture and before the Industrial Revolution, humans behaved much like other natural predators; like wolves and lions, they worked in packs to hunt elk, buffalo, deer, rabbits, and other woodland animals and did so for survival. Humans existed as part of the natural order, respecting the land and all its inhabitants. That is until they began establishing settlements and no longer hunted; instead, they began to trap, breed, and kill animals in mass numbers, disrupting the natural balance of Earth and all the creatures on it.

From the vantage points of the sky and canopy, birds and climbing critters could see animals bred for human use and consumption. They no longer hunted animals for food as they once did; they were instead breeding animals for food, keeping them trapped in pens and cages and using their skin and fur in mass quantities. For some humans, hunting became a greedy game, killing for fun and sport.

What the animals found most fascinating in watching the human species was that their only natural predator seemed to be, well, themselves. They weren't fighting one another for food sources or water, of which they had easy access and abundance to share with one another; but rather, and quite simply it seemed, for the mere sake of conflict.

Moreover, amidst plenty, they witnessed the plight of their own kind—starving, thirsty, and exposed to the elements—while others lived in opulence, indifferent to the suffering around them. Such disregard for their own kind puzzled the observing animals, who, guided by instinct, prioritized the well-being of their community, especially the vulnerable.

While humans made up a measly six percent of all mammalian species on Earth, their virulent nature was causing massive destruction around the globe, from deforestation to invasive water systems that wreaked havoc on marshland critters' habitats. So much so that the animals began to take great interest in watching this unique species that were breeding faster than wildlife creatures could keep up with.

Meanwhile, as humans remained distracted by the constant newsfeeds and stories of the horrors taking place across the globe, fighting amongst one another, competing with one another, an insidious force was slowly, silently growing. In the shadows, this force was taking control of humans and their impulses, right under their noses. Some of the animals decided it was time to fight back.

This is their story.

Part I: The Awakening

Caleb

Caleb couldn't remember life outside the lab.

Had he been born here?

His only memories were within this cell: the sterile smell and constant humming of the lights overhead, white walls and cold floors. His only companions were figures clad in white lab coats, their faces obscured behind face masks, some adorned in maroon scrubs, drifting in and out like specters throughout the day. They would administer injections that left him feeling enervated and unsettled; they wrapped a cuff around his arm and attached wires with adhesive circles to his temples and his chest. Red, blue, and green, they dangled around him.

Trapped and frightened, he learned swiftly that resistance only invited further sedation, each dose inducing a slumber filled with restless dreams and waking headaches, accompanied by waves of nausea and lethargy.

Once a week a man in a lab coat and face mask would enter his cell with a briefcase and a folding chair, setting them up at the round table in the center of his cell room. Each time the man retrieved a laptop, a deck of flashcards, a notepad, a handheld recorder, and small rubber animal figurines. With gentle yet calculated movements, he guided Caleb through a series of tasks, prompting him to identify shapes and words on the flashcards, and to categorize the animal figurines into distinct piles.

"Can you do that for me, Caleb," he would ask softly through his mask. His eyes seemed kind, but behind them, Caleb could sense malevolence.

As Caleb would perform this sorting ritual the man would speak into his recorder, making observations about his behavior.

"Day 74 post-implantation: subject appears to be instinctively separating species by classification. I am confident that we are observing 8th grade level comprehension, faster than our original projections; we are pleased with his progress."

The man looked over towards the large mirror on the wall to their right. He did this often, Caleb observed, and would even speak to his own reflection as if speaking to someone who wasn't there. The mirror was the size of the entire wall itself. The man would laugh and speak words of excitement towards his reflection, throwing 'thumbs-up' or 'high-five' motions towards the mirror. This frightened Caleb.

"Signs of sentience and verbal comprehension are rapid," he continued, his tone betraying a hint of excitement. "The first subject without signs of active rejection. I would like to recommend advancing him to literary comprehension during the next upload."

In one recurring vision, he stood before a sea of youthful faces, imparting knowledge with a fervor that seemed to transcend the confines of his cell. Upon awakening, he would find himself enriched with newfound understanding: ecosystems and animal taxonomy, meteorological phenomena and biological transformations, the distinction between amphibians and mammals, and the cosmic dance of planets in a solar system. Though he had never glimpsed the light of day, he knew the cardinal directions, the fluidity of water in its various states, and the immutable rhythm of day and night.

Despite the confines of his existence, Caleb's mind expanded beyond the sterile walls of the lab, reaching for truths that lay beyond his tangible, four-walled reality.

Every day he would wake up and know more than the day before. He understood numbers and patterns and could perform math problems in his head. His mind was flooded with mathematical scenarios that he felt compelled to solve. Alone in his cell, he would stare at the objects around his room and obsessively count and categorize them in his head. Seven rubber balls, two of which were blue, one was yellow, three were orange, and one was green. He already knew that there were sixteen flashcards, each with a unique symbol on one side, and would practice predicting the symbol for each as he flipped them, finding his predictions grew more accurate as he counted the symbols that had already gone by.

Caleb heard the buzzing sound outside his cell door that meant someone was about to enter. It was a triggering sound, knowing what to expect: more injections, flashcards, wooden blocks, or animal figurines.

This time, however, it was not just the man in the white coat who came in: with him were three other men, all holding tablet devices. The man was mid-sentence as they shuffled in, one after the other. They laughed among themselves at whatever was said, one patting the man jovially on the shoulder as they turned into the room. Then, hands on his hips, one of the new men turned towards Caleb with an eerie smile.

"So, this is the Chimp we've all been hearing about?"

Hunter

Hunter, a fifteen-pound tabby cat with a spirit as bold as his frame, ascended swiftly through the ranks of the Animal Alliance during the tumultuous dawn of the Great Event. Tales of his valor echoed through the Kingdom, yet few knew of his humble origins as a solitary housecat nestled in the suburbs outside Philadelphia.

Hunter lived in a nice, warm and comfortable house with his owners, Henry and Faith, who left him alone for many hours each day to go to work in the city. Days drifted by in a haze of solitude, punctuated only by the occasional rustle of the nearby park beyond his windowsill perch. With burnt orange fur adorned by delicate white markings, including a distinctive "ballroom glove" gracing his left front paw, Hunter cut a striking figure against the backdrop of domestic mundanity.

Hunter couldn't remember life outside the walls of his house, having been adopted as a kitten, and he felt more and more as if he were living in a prison with each passing day. From the windows he could faintly hear the songs of the birds outside, see dogs being walked leashed, who barked at one another as they passed. Occasionally groups of children walked by, carrying backpacks, laughing and chattering away, oblivious to his watching silhouette in the window.

The man in the home, Henry, liked to make the woman, Faith, laugh by grabbing Hunter with rough hands in an attempt to make him 'moonwalk.' Henry would pick him up by his armpits and drag his back legs across the floor. The joke was that there once lived a singer and dancer named Michael Jackson who wore just one glove when performing and had made infamous this dance move that made him look as if he were gliding backwards across the stage. Hunter remained unamused by Henry's roughhousing, as it hurt his underarms and left him physically sore and somewhat humiliated afterward.

Yet despite the occasional indignities, Hunter found solace in the small gestures of care from his humans—meals served, litter box tended, and a warm bed provided. Their absences, though frequent, afforded him moments of respite from the monotony of domestic life. Only in their presence did he feel the sting of neglect, their preoccupation with screens and gadgets leaving him a mere afterthought in their bustling world.

One early spring day as Hunter pondered the monotony of his life, a solitary figure caught his eye—a dark gray labradoodle, wandering with purposeful grace across the green expanse opposite his window. No collar, no leash, or human in sight. Just she alone, standing attentively with her nose pointed to the sky. She was sniffing the air, not the ground, as he had observed other dogs do, their noses hovering frantically just above the grass, occasionally burrowing them into the dirt itself.

As he observed her movements, Hunter's ears perked up and eyes dilated to bring in more light. His instinct told him to pay close attention to this strangely behaving dog. He slowly positioned himself from crouched on all fours to sitting upright and at attention, front paws digging into the back of the chair alongside his hindquarters. His whiskers shuddered as he directed his focus on her every movement. She wasn't running or panting, but rather walking calmly with her tail in a relaxed position. He had never observed a dog whose body language appeared so calm yet so alert at the same time, attentive to its surroundings but neither skittish nor anxious.

This labradoodle's behavior was, therefore, of exceptional interest to Hunter. After realizing one of his paws was starting to fall asleep in his concentration, he again settled onto all fours, ready to observe for hours if necessary.

Hunter noticed a rhythm to her movements. She walked around the perimeter of the park, lowering her head from time to time, sniffing intentionally and slowly, as if on some sort of mission. After pawing the ground a bit, she lifted her head upright again, walking towards the center of the green with the intentionality and poise of a show dog, but with no audience in sight.

His attention peaked when the labradoodle's gaze momentarily met his own, sending a jolt of apprehension coursing through him. Ducking low to avoid detection, Hunter observed as she deftly retrieved a crushed can, her movements fluid and precise. With careful determination, she navigated towards a nearby birch tree, her mission clear yet enigmatic.

She slowed down as she approached the branch birch tree, eventually stopping in front of a rough white and gray rock at the base of the tree. Balancing the can atop the rough rock with delicate precision, the labradoodle exhibited a quiet determination, her actions imbued with a sense of purpose. Hunter watched in silent awe as she meticulously arranged the makeshift offering, her canine instincts guiding her every move.

As she retreated from her handiwork, Hunter remained rooted to his spot, his curiosity piqued by the mysterious ritual he had just witnessed. Hours passed as he lingered by the window, his thoughts consumed by the enigmatic labradoodle and the silent bond they shared, tethered by a momentary exchange of gazes and a shared understanding of the world beyond their confines.

Beatrice

Beatrice was a squirrel who, as she was told by her family and community, was born with a gift. She could decipher human code. And not just written code: at a young age she started noticing the signs put up by humans with symbols and colors used along roadways. After observing the movements of the cars, she realized that these signs and lights created a kind of language for the cars and their passengers.

Beatrice unraveled how these signs created traffic patterns and organized behaviors for the cars that allowed them to travel at irregular velocities, at speeds that were unfathomable to the animals. Squirrels had the highest mortality rate when it came to humans and their cars. While squirrels could not communicate verbally like humans, they had several nonverbal forms of communication that they had developed over the years, including using various chirps, squeaks, and tail-flicking motions to add emphasis when needed.

Developed over the last century, these squirrels managed to keep their secret from most other animals, or so they assumed. Considered a prophet of sorts by her community, Beatrice was born in the city of Boston, Massachusetts. She had only ever known living among humans. Taught at a young age the secrets of avoiding cars and handsy children, Beatrice had mastered the art of climbing and navigating the city via their various wires hanging above the city lights.

Furthermore, she studied the sounds of cars honking and accelerating, a familiar cacophony that she used to map her way across busy intersections or avoid distracted pedestrians. Their eyes were locked on their phones and were unaware of her scurrying by their feet to grab discarded and unclaimed breakfast as the rushing commuters popped in and out of the subway entrances.

While her siblings kept their focus on avoiding the dangers of mingling with these humans, Beatrice would spend hours studying their behavior. More than once, she had witnessed the deaths of friends who had miscalculated a car's maneuver around a corner or hovered too long over the train tracks.

The first time she had witnessed a death was that of her mother's good friend. She had tried to cross the road after nearby squirrel watchers gave her the go-ahead. She did not see that a cyclist was speeding her way as she started her passage across the asphalt. It was too late. Beatrice saw the man hurtling towards her, sitting upright on his bicycle wearing a backpack, hands not on the handlebars but instead gripping his cell phone and texting. Not a car in sight, his attention was exclusively on his phone, and he was completely unaware of the squirrel crossing the road in front of him.

His victim's attention, however, was fixed upon the grassy knoll on the other side of the street. She became aware of him but assumed he would swerve around her, like most cyclists. Her first, and last, mistake was to trust a human who had his attention on something else. As he was looking down at his phone his front wheel managed to run over her back legs and hips. She heard and felt her bones crunch, the pain searing up her spine and down her arms. She dug her claws into the asphalt, one of them tearing away from her finger from her efforts. Then, making it not more than a foot in front of her, her head fell to the ground, twitching in pain until, finally, she lay lifeless on the pavement.

More than the image of her mangled body on the road, Beatrice remembered the face of the man who killed her mother's friend; looking back in annoyance and indifference as he righted himself on his bike and carried on with the same nonchalance as if he had run over a beer can. In this moment she had a revelation: these humans are truly dangerous. They were ignorant of their violence, and unphased and unbothered by their destructive behavior. Beatrice gradually became numb to the increasing deaths happening around her.

As the seasons shifted, Beatrice bore witness to the escalating toll of human negligence, her once vibrant community dwindling in the face of their destructive apathy. Death by violence became an expected part of life as a metropolitan squirrel.

Beatrice, while in the commons one day, noticed a swan in the lake staring at her. At first, she thought she was imagining it, but soon realized the swan was intentionally locking eyes with her; it was as if she had something important that she needed to tell Beatrice. They held each other's gaze for an uncomfortable amount of time, the swan's eyes simultaneously hypnotic and terrifying to behold. Beatrice could not look away.

Cadillac

Cadillac was less than a year old when her owner, Roland, adopted her. She didn't remember much of her early months, other than feeling overwhelmed by all the sounds and smells of the shelter. Terrified by the loud noises and confused by the cacophony of smells around her, she held onto the memory of her mother for comfort: the smell of her soft fur, the sound of her breath, and the rhythm of her heartbeat. Aside from that of her mother's fur, the smell she loved most was Roland's cologne. They became best friends very quickly, though she found him rather strict at first.

Cadillac had been born in the shelter to her mother, a labradoodle mix brought in anonymously to the shelter who, upon receiving medical care, was found to be six weeks pregnant with four pups. Roland was a 77 year-old retired professor. He had taught Astrophysics at a university outside of Buffalo, New York for twenty-three years, previously having worked for NASA.

She could hear him down the corridor meeting with a couple of other dogs. His voice was low and barely audible, while the other voice was loud, high and bubbly, as they went back and forth about the dogs he was visiting. She heard foot-steps and voices approaching and saw Roland approach her cage alongside a uniformed volunteer. Shy and apprehensive at first, as she was still traumatized from her experiences with being in-troduced to boisterous children who pulled and tugged at her fur and tail too roughly, Cadillac quickly warmed up to Roland. In a comforting gesture he slowly squatted down, gently adjusting his brown trousers and cream-colored button up shirt as he met her face-to-face at her level. He didn't reach out to pet her or try to tussle her ears. He warmly said, "Hello, I am Roland. Nice to meet you."

Cadillac remembered the long drive from the shelter to Roland's home. She trembled in the back seat, but he didn't fuss over her. He put on music and quietly hummed along. His eyes were mostly fixed on the road but, occasionally, she would catch him adjusting the rear-view mirror so he could look back at her to make sure she was okay. She whimpered and shook, but he just continued humming to the music, reaching his arm back while keeping his head forward and focused on driving so that he could gently touch her paw. This brought her great comfort.

Arriving at their destination, Cadillac's eyes widened in awe as she beheld Roland's home—a sprawling two-story cot-tage ensconced within lush gardens and towering trees. It was a haven of tranquility, a sanctuary awaiting her timid arrival.

As Roland opened the door for her, he motioned towards the ground, inviting her to exit, then walked toward his house. With a gentle internal nudge, she stepped out of the car, head between her shoulders and tail tucked between her legs. From outside of the car, Cadillac could see Roland sitting in a chair on the porch holding a book, legs crossed and reading intently. By his feet was a small plate with food on it. The door of the house had been left ajar, an invitation for her to join him.

Cadillac walked slowly toward the house, looking from side to side and then back up towards Roland again. The grass was soft and spongy against her paws, a sensation she had not experienced before. She sniffed at it and became overwhelmed by all the new scents she was experiencing. At the shelter, she was brought outside daily and was taken on short walks, but the ground was never as soft and lush as this; it always smelled overwhelmingly of other dogs' urine and feces. This grass smelled sweet, so much so that she had an overwhelming urge to eat it.

Roland continued reading, glancing up from his book from time to time to check her progress; a smile seemed to linger just behind his lips even as he was looking down as if he was watching her without watching her. Cadillac wasn't sure how much time had passed but eventually found herself up on the porch next to him. She looked at the food next to him, then up at him. He smiled warmly at her and nodded, as if to say, 'Go ahead, it's all yours,' then continued reading. She sniffed the plate and its contents and began salivating. She took a small bite and was overwhelmed by all the flavors she was experiencing. She ate slowly and mindfully and, as she ate, felt his strong hand pat her gently on her left hip. This was a familiar feeling. She remembered again what love felt like.

15

When his life felt especially empty, and to stave off the loneliness trying to take hold, Roland would call Cadillac to join him on the couch and read to her from his favorite books. His worn copies of Carl Sagan's *Cosmos* or Stephen Hawking's *A Brief History of Time* still incited his passion for his calling, and he often paused mid-chapter to talk through some passages, speaking to Cadillac as if lecturing his students, mostly for his own amusement. Cadillac lay by his side, sprawled out, often sighing with boredom and disappointment that he was giving this book all his attention instead of gently patting her sides and shoulders.

After eight years of his walks and astronomy lessons, Cadillac began to retain the information Roland was sharing with her. Of course, she had no way to effectively verbalize to him that she could comprehend every word he was saying, but she used her facial expressions and body language to express her excitement in her ability to understand him. "Do you want dinner?" he would ask and she, eager to respond, would wag her tail and back legs vigorously with excitement, licking her lips from the instant salivation that started as soon as she heard the word 'dinner'. "Yes, yes, yes!" she would exclaim non-verbally. She learned that trying to vocalize with her barking was met with a firm scolding from Roland. "I need to know when you are trying to protect me. Save your barks for me and stop wasting them on the squirrels," he would jest.

Once a week, Roland would summon Cadillac for a car ride. Leash in hand he would lead her to the car and open the back door for her (she was not allowed in the front seat). Roland always had music on, whether driving or doing dishes or even when reading in the evenings before bed. But on this ride, he never put music on. Cadillac learned not to disturb him during this drive and would lay solemnly in the back seat. She knew they were going to visit his stone that he called 'Eloise,' her anticipation tempered by the somberness of the occasion.

As they arrived, Roland would park the car, then sit in silence for a few moments before emerging. Only then would Cadillac stir, waiting until she heard the car door open before moving. With a click, Roland would fasten the leash to her collar, and together they'd navigate the field of stones.

She saw the stone named Eloise and kept her head down, waiting for Roland to kneel in front of it as he always did. She was not to disturb him during their conversation.

"Hello, my love," he always greeted her.

He had long conversations with her while Cadillac lay on the ground next to him, unable to watch him. Often, tears would stream down his face. She could feel that he was in great pain, but there was nothing she could do except stay by his side while he suffered.

Roland liked to talk to her about her gardens. Cadillac learned through their visits that Eloise was an avid gardener and had grown a splendid backyard haven for them when they lived together. In bloom every season except winter, her perennial flowers were expertly staggered to make sure there was always a living canvas of blossoms blessing their property. While Roland hadn't done much gardening himself, he still enjoyed sitting with her while she toiled in the soil.

"I should have taken you to England," Cadillac remembered him telling Eloise once, his hand braced against the stone. Apparently, she spoke often of her desire to travel to England just to experience its illustrious gardens.

"I wouldn't need to go anywhere else," he remembered she used to say. "Just bring me to the gardens and serve me tea – and have an umbrella close at hand just in case."

He began to sob uncontrollably, gasping for air. "Oh Eloise, I don't know who I am without you."

Roland was kneeling on the ground now, his knees wet and dirty, crying into his hands. Cadillac became scared. She couldn't tell if he was breathing. Leaping up she began to lick his face, but he shoved her down aggressively, telling her to stay away. Her heart broke, confused by his anger. He brought her back to the car, opened the backseat door and, to her surprise, got into the backseat with her. He closed the door gently, looking at her tenderly and with remorse, then embraced her around her shoulders, sobbing into the soft curly fur of her neck. She leaned her head against his and let him cry.

Sally

Sally, a cocker-spaniel, resided in a lavish Manhattan loft with her owner, April, a former Instagram influencer turned celebrity. Elevated by April's fame, Sally herself had amassed a substantial following on social media, boasting an Instagram account adorned with glamorous photos showcasing her pampered lifestyle: grooming sessions, designer accessories, and chic ensembles.

Her fame grew as Sally appeared on daytime television shows and suddenly, she and April were being booked for a plethora of events. Sally had even been invited to attend a Fashion Week extravaganza! Sitting prettily by April's stilettoed feet, she watched the models' stoic and fierce faces break into girlish smiles as they waved to the canine showstopper. Unable to contain their gushing grins, they looked down adoringly at her from the runway, poised luxuriously in her Louis Vuitton dog tote, in a matching LV doggie cardigan and collar, ears freshly washed and trimmed.

Within a few months, April had landed a book deal. Many of her social media posts were centered around Sally's specialized diet, as she suffered from irritable bowel syndrome, a rare occurrence in dogs that left April having to do a lot of trial and error with Sally's diet. As a result, April started preparing meals for Sally to accommodate her sensitive stomach and received an outpouring of support from other dog owners whose pups also shared Sally's diagnosis. Her foodie posts became so popular that her fans begged for her recipes, demanding she author a cookbook.

April found herself a publisher and got to work, and in no time her Canine Cookery Book was a huge success. April was asked to do a book tour and, with Sally in tow, traveled around the country for book signings and cooking demos on cable networks: from CNN to The Food Network, Sally was a nationwide celebrity and exulted in all the attention she received. All the cooking shows scrambled to book Sally to try special gourmet meals prepared by their best signature chefs. Their live audiences cheered as they watched the pretty little spaniel daintily lap up five-star meals fashioned especially for her.

While on the road, Sally languished in the luxuries of four-star hotel living. Groomers were brought to her room, and she received pet massages every week, as well as various naturopathic treatments to relieve her sensitive stomach and skin. While Sally enjoyed all these amenities, April had become consumed with her own celebrity status and now spent most of her time networking at posh events lasting into the early morning hours. More and more frequently, Sally was left alone in her hotel room while April enjoyed evenings devoid of her dog-owner responsibilities.

April's personal assistant and the hotel staff were instructed to check in on Sally, but they really did not interact with her at all. Left to her own devices, Sally grew increasingly restless and lonely in the confines of her room. She yearned for the attention of her fans and the companionship of April during their outings. Exploring every nook of her limited space, Sally eventually settled by a window, watching the bustling activity below to pass the time. Envious of other dogs being walked by their owners, Sally longed for the social interactions she once enjoyed.

Before April's book deal, Sally relished long walks and trips to the dog park with her owner. They used to have dedicated photo shoots together in the park. However, with April's newfound celebrity status, Sally was relegated to the company of a hired dog walker who showed little enthusiasm for their outings. Deprived of socializing opportunities and the sensory delights of outdoor exploration, Sally's loneliness deepened. Though she enjoyed the perks of her celebrity status, such as the attention and travel, Sally missed the simple joys of interacting with other dogs and indulging in the scents of nature, especially the tempting aromas of discarded treats left by passersby.

Sometimes, Sally heard other dogs barking in the hotel and would call back to them, feeling a kinship in their shared loneliness. She yearned for companionship and longed to invite them to her room to play.

It was during a particularly rainy day in Philadelphia, cooped up in a hotel room alone once again, that Sally's nose picked up a new and unfamiliar whiff of something. Her keen sense of smell led her to a closet by the entryway, where the odor seemed strongest. Sniffing vigorously along the bottom of the door, Sally tried to identify what lay on the other side. Startled by a movement, she jumped back, but her curiosity soon overcame her fear.

Once her adrenaline subsided, her curiosity overruled her fear and Sally pawed at the base of the door, trying to see if that would cause whatever was in the closet to move again. She crouched down, her head tilting against the floor to try to see under the small crack underneath the closet and, for a second, she saw a flash of dull fur. She jumped back in surprise, but then quickly got back into her watchful stance, rump in the air and nose to the ground. What was this creature and why was it in their room?

The closet had sliding doors and Sally attempted to paw one open, but it was much too heavy for her. She tried digging at the floor and even laid down on her side, using all four paws in a running motion to try and pry it open. She had no luck and was mortified to notice she had accidentally left scratch marks on the door and floor.

"Hopefully April won't notice," she thought. She paced back and forth, then tried to paw at the door some more, then more pacing until she finally gave up her efforts, but not her vigilance: she lay on the floor by the closet, waiting, sighing and flicking her tail with impatience. She hoped that when April came back, she might open this door, and Sally could dash in to investigate.

Finally, Sally perked up at the sound of a hotel key card beeping outside the door, hoping it was April coming to open the closet. Disappointed, she realized it was only April's assistant, Charles, arriving to take her for a walk. Despite needing to relieve herself, Sally hesitated to leave her post, fearing the creature might return.

Jabbering on, he grabbed Sally's leash and hooked it to her harness, shushing her out the door as she shook her fur to adjust her harness. Trembling from holding her bladder, Sally eagerly relieved herself on the grass outside. Yet, her mind remained on the mysterious visitor in the closet. She began walking back to the hotel, Charles surprised that she didn't want to walk around a bit more, but also relieved that his dog-duties were done

Once upstairs, he unleashed her and promptly left. She could hear his voice grower fainter, still on the phone, as he walked back down towards the elevators. She carefully approached the closet door and was caught off guard, stopping dead in her tracks: just outside the closet door, on the floor where she had been lying prior to her walk, she saw that something had taken her leftover breakfast bits out of her dish and arranged them in a tidy circle.

Sam

Sam the groundhog, like most groundhogs, was a loner. It's true that while most groundhogs are known to be cautious and home-bodies, Sam was a little less so, but he was still apprehensive of venturing too far from this field. Collaborating with other groundhogs, Sam and his kin constructed a network of tunnels beneath the meadow, providing safe passage and access to food without attracting predators.

From the tunnels in the meadow, they could access vegetation and insects for food without risking being seen and hunted by nearby foxes or bears. Overall, they weren't a social group; most spent their days grazing and sunbathing in dirt patches in and among the tall wheat grass. Occasionally one might venture out a bit further beyond their territory to reconnoiter for new, more exciting food: wild raspberries, chrysanthemums or other out-of-the-ordinary treats that didn't naturally grow nearby.

Sam spent most of his days alone, minus the occasional interactions he shared in passing with other animals. Often, however, he would choose to hide before they could engage with him, as he was not much for socializing. So that is why one morning, when he heard panicked yelping from beyond the trees, he was confused by his urge to run towards the ruckus, and not away. His impulse was to help, not to hide, which was new to him as well. The frantic distress cries were like none he had ever heard before and sent shivers down his spine.

Sam found his legs taking him past the north edge of the meadow, away from the others and further away from his own den than he had ever ventured before. As he neared the perimeter of the meadow the sounds of the screaming grew louder. At first, he thought it might be some kind of fox or wolf in distress, but they usually didn't carry on this long as such carrying on would be sure to draw attention from predators and even birds of prey, ready to swoop in once the deed was done. This noise, however, continued and grew in intensity, not a cry of pain, no he thought. It was a cry for help.

Unsure what help, if any, he might provide, Sam still felt compelled to push forward. He paused intermittently, hoping the cries would stop so he could retreat, but his newfound conscience compelled him to advance toward the distress cries. He navigated through the woods, hopping over fallen branches, popping behind trees for cover and, finally, came to an opening at the wood's edge. He peeked over a tree stump that stood just outside the perimeter of the forest and from there he saw a house surrounded by gardens.

Sam had known some groundhogs who were bold enough to trespass on humans' land to forage through their yards, especially those with gardens such as these. He had heard rumors of the humans' wrath, and how taking the bounty of their gardens was punishable by death, so he personally never thought the risk worthwhile.

He sat at the edge of the woods, debating if he should approach the house. Every instinctive fiber in his being was telling him to turn around and run but, for some unfathomable reason his impulse was to make a mad dash for the nearest lilac bush to get a closer look. He had come this far with no signs of danger and his curiosity compelled him to complete his quest.

Assessing the area, Sam's eyes darted back and forth as they scanned for predators. He lowered himself as close to the ground as he could, scurrying in a zig-zag pattern towards the lilacs. From underneath the tall lilac shrubs he was able to get a better view of the house and could even see into some of the windows. He pulled himself upright on both hind legs, supporting his upper body on the roots of the shrubs which grew up out of the ground, and observed.

Now within earshot of the unrelenting howling and crashing noises emanating from the house, Sam dashed towards its foundation, seeking refuge under the cover of large Hosta plants. From this hidden vantage point, nestled among the broad leaves, he could peer into a window and observe the chaotic movements inside.

The curtains rustled every so often, as if someone were running in circles, sweeping the curtains against the window-panes. Sam was staring so intently at the glass that, when the dog inside began throwing itself at the window, he became startled;

he fell backwards over himself, breaking a couple of the Hosta leaves in the process.

Recovering his composure, Sam cautiously repositioned himself, peering over the leaves, waiting for the dog's next move. Suddenly, the tumult ceased, the curtains stilled, and the barking subsided. Uncertain of his next steps, Sam pondered his limited options. How could a mere groundhog possibly aid a distressed dog trapped inside a house?

It was obvious that something was not right inside the house. If only the dog would look out and see him, they could acknowledge one another and, perhaps, Sam could let her know that, while helpless, he was aware she was in distress. He decided that if he were similarly distressed, it would comfort him to know that he was not alone.

In truth, Sam realized his options were limited; returning home seemed the most sensible course of action. With his adrenaline subsiding, hunger gnawed at him, and he couldn't ignore the tantalizing vegetation surrounding him in the gardens. Despite brief hesitation over potential human encounters, Sam's rumbling stomach won out, especially considering the absence of any apparent human presence due to the dog's behavior inside the house.

Lost in his observations of the house's commotion, Sam hadn't fully appreciated the beauty of his surroundings. Examining the gardens more closely, he discovered an array of flowers and shrubs in various stages of growth. Coneflowers, Chrysan-themums, and Russian Sage bordered ornamental trees, with morning glories weaving between structures, their petals poised to unfurl in the daylight. Flowers were a delicacy for ground-hogs, especially those who lived mainly in the forest where such foliage did not grow naturally.

Overcome by his hunger, Sam lumbered slowly over to some of the phlox that had started to bloom and began to nibble away. He paused from time to time to look back at the window, hoping he might catch a glimpse of the dog again. As he worked through his guilt of eating so gloriously while there was a dog trapped inside in need of help, he heard a loud rustling beyond the tree line behind him.

Every muscle in his body tensed, and the tasty morsels he had been chewing dropped to the ground. Crouched low, he watched as a black bear burst from the woods, almost galloping toward the house. Sam couldn't believe his eyes as the bear, with purpose, approached, seized an ornamental glass ball, and hurled it through the closest window, shattering the glass. After a brief pause, the bear turned and loped back into the woods. Unsure of what to do next, Sam focused intently on the broken window, anticipating the dog's escape.

Spotting a large shard of broken glass hanging from the window frame, Sam felt compelled to warn the dog of the po-tential hazard. Rushing toward the window, he hoped his pres-ence alone might steady her, preventing injury in her desperation to escape.

By the time the dog reached the broken window, Sam was already right outside of it, waiting in anticipation for her to make her escape. The dog was panting heavily, fur matted and wet from a steady stream of drool running down her neck. What Sam noticed most about the dog was her striking bright yellow eyes against her gray curly fur, her face full of terror and desperation. But as the dog paced back and forth in front of the window, Sam could see her assessing an escape route with mindfulness.

Without fully understanding why, Sam calmly positioned himself in the dog's line of sight. They held each other's gaze momentarily, and to convey his intent, Sam used his paws to carefully clear away sharp pieces of glass from the ground, ensuring her safe passage upon escape.

Cadillac

One Fall morning Cadillac woke up to find Roland missing from his bed. Nor was his bedding mussed, as he typically left it disheveled until after their morning garden jaunt, when he was sufficiently caffeinated to make the bed. Concerned, she rose immediately and darted out to the living room. There she found Roland in his favorite leather chair, appearing asleep at first, but his head and shoulders were awkwardly and unnaturally slumped over, his head dangling over his lap. Occasionally he had been known to fall asleep reading in his chair, but never through an entire night and certainly not in this unnatural position. Startled to see him this way, Cadillac immediately trotted over to him, a whine escaping her muzzle, with no reaction from Roland.

Cadillac desperately jumped up and pawed at Roland's legs, hoping to startle him into sitting upright. But her frantic efforts only caused him to slump further into his own lap. Panicked, she scratched at his legs, tearing his pants and leaving scratch marks down his shins, but Roland remained motionless. Her scratching escalated into vigorous digging, causing his body to shift and pitch forward towards the floor. Cadillac watched in horror as Roland fell, crumpled face down onto the floor.

Terrified, she began tugging at his old white T-shirt and flannel pajama pants to try and rouse him, which just caused one of the pant legs to tear away completely from his calf, revealing the damage she had done to his body. Whimpering and shrieking, she ran back and forth from one end of the house to the other, knocking over picture frames from side tables and books from their cases. She began purposefully pulling at the curtains, shattering the small porcelain bird collectibles kept on the windowsill near his chair in the process. She was desperately hoping to draw somebody's attention to the house, someone who could help her beloved owner. But the nearest neighbor was more than a half-mile down the road, and she was stuck behind solid wooden locked doors, unable to push any of them open despite her best efforts. After more than two hours of searching for an escape, her vocal cords were weary and raw from barking and shrieking. Capitulated, she slumped over his body, panting in exhaustion; forlorn, terrified, and devastated.

Roland was gone.

Panting heavily, collapsed next to Roland, Cadillac's tongue hung from her mouth onto the floor. She could feel the coolness of the hardwood against her pulsing tongue, pressing her shoulder and hips against the cold floor to help soothe her exhausted body. She turned her eyes to look at her owner, his body slumped unnaturally against the floor, and Cadillac began to cry. Roland was gone.

Cadillac laid there for a long time, wondering how she could live without him. Cadillac anxiously recounted the shelter where she had been born and taken from her mother. As panicked as she felt, she could only muster up the strength to whimper. She was unsure of how much time had passed but was aware of hunger pangs starting in her belly but did not have the energy or desire to get up and find food.

What would she do without Roland? He fed her, took her to the doctor, groomed her, comforted her and, most importantly, he loved her. Cadillac decided against moving at all and settled her solid body next to Roland's, feeling the warmth of his body gradually leave him. She became possessive of him; she was fearful someone might try to take him away. Despite her fears, she eventually fell into an exhausted sleep, taking in the last whiffs of his cologne that she loved so much.

Startled awake by a loud crash from the kitchen, Cadillac sprang into action, her claws clicking on the smooth wooden floor as she scrambled to investigate. Upon entering the kitchen, she found one of the decorative marble garden orbs chipped and broken in half on the floor by the sink, surrounded by shards of glass. Taking in the scene before her, she could feel a refreshing breeze coming through the window, cool and damp. Without hesitation she sprang up onto the counter, her feet slipping and scrambling along the basin sink, trembling to lift herself atop the counter to look outside.

As she gazed through the large hole in the window apparently made by the orb, the first thing she saw, aside from broken glass scattered everywhere, was a groundhog. The small animal was brown with dark-brown tipped ears and was holding a larger piece of glass between his tiny black fingers. He stopped what he was doing immediately, looking straight at her. She held eye contact with him, not feeling compelled to bark but baffled by this unusual exchange. While the groundhog looked equally perplexed, he placidly continued picking up and moving glass away from the porch below, even using his back legs to brush some of the smaller pieces aside.

Cadillac's fight or flight impulse had subsided enough at this point so that she did not immediately jump out of the now-shattered window. Seeing this groundhog acting so out of character helped to center her as she was able to pause and assess the situation at hand. They both sensed at once that they were now working together towards a common goal: the dog's escape. So, the groundhog continued quickly but carefully to push aside glass as Cadillac worked in tandem with her nose and paws to carefully clear out the sharp edges still hanging from the wooden frames.

The shattered pane offered Cadillac an easy escape route once she had cleared away the glass. Balancing precariously on her hind legs in the sink, she braced herself against the window-sill and propelled herself forward, her front paws preparing for the impact below. However, in her haste, she caught her back right paw on the ledge, scratching it as she descended. Surprised by the stinging sensation, she landed awkwardly on her side, struggling to regain her footing due to the ache in her hips from the fall.

Stunned, she sat up and approached the groundhog. She lowered her head as if to say, 'thank you,' and he, not knowing what else to do, returned the gesture. As she stood over the groundhog, Cadillac pondered the unusual circumstances, considering whether he had witnessed the event or played a role in her escape. However, she dismissed the latter possibility, unable to fathom how such a small creature could shatter a window. After a silent exchange, the groundhog scurried away, leaving Cadillac standing on the porch, contemplating her next move.

Cadillac stood on the porch staring at the trees where she had seen her friend disappear for a long while and it wasn't until she became aware of mosquitos buzzing in her face that she was brought back into her reality.

Not knowing what else to do, other than knowing she did not want to go back inside the house, Cadillac walked towards the trees. She knew if she stayed in the house, waiting for someone to find Roland, that she would end up back at the shelter.

She did not want to go back there. So, it seemed, the forest was her best option.

Phillip

Phillip Masterson, a human, worked as an Earth Science teacher for middle-school students. Growing up in a middle-class neighborhood, he navigated the dynamics of an overbearing mother and an emotionally absent workaholic father. With two younger siblings, one still in high school and the other in his sophomore year at Boston University, Phillip's family life shaped his early years.

Phillip never had much of a social life during high school, and it wasn't until college that he started making actual friends. He felt awkward around his classmates and self-conscious in general, especially when it came to his transgender identity, something he was fortunate to learn at a young and privileged enough to have parents and a community supporting him through his transition.

But he did not like the attention it brought him; it left him feeling like a mascot of sorts. In college he got way too many 'hey bro!'s from the guys in class, going out of their way to try and engage him in hyper-masculine conversation, as if they were trying to teach him how to be 'a real man.' More challenging than the guys he had befriended over the years were the women: from high school through college, he was notoriously perceived as 'the best guy friend,' but rarely did any of them show interest beyond making out.

There was nothing dramatic about Phillip's life that drew attention to him. No features that set him apart from others that were worth praising or even ridiculing; not unkempt but not stylish either, he managed to avoid the popularity game by sketching or writing just far enough away from classmates so that he did not seem intimidated by them, nor did he appear a loner, incapable of socializing.

Phillip's fascination with science, particularly Earth Science, ignited at a young age. The boundless complexity of Earth's ecosystems and the myriad unanswered questions they posed captivated him deeply. This passion steered his career choice; fresh out of college, he saw teaching as a means to influence the next wave of scientists, especially amidst mounting concerns like climate change, pandemics, and natural disasters. His goal was clear: to equip students with a scientific understanding of these issues, countering the prevalent misinformation perpetuated through social media and sensationalized news.

Phillip lived in Los Angeles with his roommate and good friend, Stephanie, whom he met while studying at the University of Southern California. Both majored in Early Childhood Education and became close when they started teaching together. While they used to spend a lot of time together, she had started dating her now girlfriend a few months back and was spending a lot of time over at her apartment, leaving Phillip home alone often. An introvert at heart, and often stretched thin after teaching a room full of hormonal pre-teens, he spent his evenings retreating to his room where he played video games for hours.

Occasionally, his gaming reverie was interrupted by his mother's phone calls, which invariably veered toward his dating life. She knew he had struggled throughout his life when it came to dating and was adamant that marriage was the solution to depression and loneliness. There had been a couple of relationships he had maintained for a few months, but he admittedly was not a great boyfriend. He didn't like to go out much and had a hard time letting his guard down and being emotionally available. So, Phillip enjoyed filling his empty hours playing online video games, which annoyed his mother to no end, as she felt strongly that he should be spending his time pursuing a long-term, romantic relationship.

"It's unhealthy," she admonished him once. "I saw an article on Facebook about how video games lead to depression and anxiety."

Phillip found solace in his video games, a refuge from the mundanc routines of his daily life. While his colleagues engaged in political debates and student grievances, he sought escape in the immersive realms of gaming. Teaching middle schoolers about Earth's intricacies drained him, especially as he battled to capture their wandering attention amidst TikTok distractions and Instagram dramas. Nonetheless, he occasionally embraced modern trends, integrating #sciencetok into his lesson plans.

KINGDOM OF BEASTS

Phillip's favorite game, *Kingdom of Beasts*, was one that had become particularly popular among young adults. He had overheard students excitedly discussing the game in the hallways between classes and, out of curiosity and the desire to relate more to the next generation, he downloaded the game on his Xbox one evening. *Kingdom of Beasts* was a role-playing game where players had the freedom to choose an avatar for themselves from various animal clans, with multiple kingdoms to explore and earn rewards as they completed various missions in service of their kingdom.

Phillip's avatar was a puma he named Jethro. For his armor, he chose the medieval themed chest and shoulder plates, and donned a kilt. In this game, he was one of many animals in an alternate reality wherein humans did not exist, and animals had all evolved into sentience simultaneously. He found the premise of *Kingdom of Beasts* to be clever, especially from a science nerd's perspective; the idea of a different version of Earth had evolution taken another turn.

Phillip often would get chat requests from online players but mostly ignored them. There were a handful of established online friends he trusted and was wary of starting conversations with people he did not know. So, he surprised himself one evening when, while stymied during a particularly complicated mission, a notification popped up informing him that someone wanted to chat with him. Impulsively, and likely due to yet another dead end rather than actual interest in the sender, he decided to accept the message.

"Hello! Would you like to form an alliance with me?"

Phillip had received anonymous invitations to join a co-op in the past, but no one had ever used the term 'alliance.' He preferred to play solo but was feeling somewhat lonely and disconnected this time and his curiosity was piqued. It was not only the content of the message that caught his attention, but also the username:

QueenOfHearts666

He thought for a minute, then responded.

"What do you mean, alliance?" he asked.

Phillip stopped everything he was doing, sat back in his chair, grabbed his Diet Coke and sipped slowly as he waited for a response. He was very aware that he was still a novice at this game and was sure that any assistance he might provide would be nominal at best. After three minutes or so he still had not received a response from QueenOfHearts666. He was ready to close the chat window and move on, assuming they had lost interest, but was suddenly compelled to say more.

"I mean, I have only been playing this game for a month or so, so I don't know how much help I could be," he followed up using his headset to dictate his chat response.

The mysterious player replied almost immediately:

"I will be heading to the Woodland Kingdom. Chapter 17. The mission with the Order of the Ruminants. We need to provide protection to their leader as they cross the Navient River."

He looked at the time: 9:37 p.m. It was still relatively early in the evening. He gazed around him and studied the state of his apartment, thinking that he should clean up a bit instead, as he had neglected the dishes for a couple of days, but found himself intrigued by this new mission.

"Ok," he responded. "I'll see you there!"

QueenOfHearts666 didn't respond but he went ahead and navigated to the mission anyway. He had not yet been to this kingdom, spending most of his gaming time in the Bulhegan Jungle with the Talon Pride, a group of cats and birds of prey at war with the reptilian group, the Squamata Allegiance. From the map landing screen, he navigated to the Woodland Kingdom and his avatar found himself near a slow-flowing river bordered by pine, oak, and birch trees.

He waited to see their avatar and, as he spun his character around, found himself face to face with a praying mantis avatar, wearing a silk flowing robe of sorts, forearms emblazoned with gold armor cuffs, decorated with indigo and ruby jewels. As he approached them, they messaged:

"Follow me," they commanded.

With his fingers gripped tightly around the controller, Phillip trailed after them. They broke into a jog, and using his analog stick, Phillip matched their pace. Ahead, the entrance to the next mission loomed, the luminescent green creature bounding across a field by the river. Yet, in a sudden sideways leap, they veered unexpectedly to the right of the target. Phillip suspected a controller mishap but noticed they weren't correcting their course. Just as he considered messaging them, a prompt appeared:

"Keep following me."

He was confused and messaged back, "But I thought the mission was straight ahead."

"This is a side quest. Just follow me," they replied.

As they turned right, the praying mantis avatar started glitching and shaking, a telltale sign of straying beyond the game's boundaries. They continued glitching, and Phillip watched as they darted back and forth along the border. Doubt crept in; perhaps this was all a prank orchestrated by a roomful of giggling preteens. Then, without warning, they vanished into the graphics, swallowed by the line of CGI trees.

Phillip stared at the screen wondering where they had disappeared to. As if in answer to his unasked question, they sent another message:

"Keep running back and forth, it will let you in."

Following their instructions, Phillip awkwardly sprinted against the tree line. After a few moments, his avatar emerged into an entirely new landscape, nothing like the game's familiar graphics. Frozen in disbelief, Phillip maneuvered Jethro to survey his surroundings.

He found himself in what resembled ancient catacombs, the colors and design starkly different from the game he had been playing moments ago.

"Keep following," they said.

So, he did.

Andean

Andean was a Black Bear who lived with her cub, Silver, in the Finger Lakes National Forest in New York.

They had a great life together. She taught him how to climb trees whose berries were edible, the art of catching fish in the stream, and the importance of good grooming habits. She also taught him how to tend to his wounds, how to care for one another when they were sick, and how to find his way home in case she was not around. They grew to become quite dependent on one another, as was common with mama bears and their cubs. She could smell Silver's unique smell from a mile away, a comforting scent of earth and oil. She would press her muzzle against the warmth of his dark fur and deeply breathe in his essence.

Sleeping at night with him tucked in her underbelly for warmth, she would try to synchronize her breathing with his, or alternate her breaths to help him learn the rhythm of his own lungs and to gauge the oxygen needs of his blood. She was training him to slow his own breathing in order to conserve energy. For bears, regulating their breath and heart rate was crucial for survival through the long New York winters; with fewer calories available to sustain their large mass, they had to train their bodies to be sedentary and efficient, through carefully controlled breath and movement.

Andean often challenged her cub to control his breathing at night in rhythm with hers: inhaling and waiting for him to do the same, holding her breath until he finished his inhale; then letting it out and giving him a little squeeze to do the same. In this way, the rhythm of their hearts and breath naturally synchronized. And, when the connection weakened from the stress of survival, such as during hibernation, they could reconnect by synchronizing their breaths. In the stillness of the dark cold nights, aware of each other's warm breath rustling the other's fur, they rediscovered each other's soul.

Silver knew that when his mother held her breath it meant she was listening. When she listened, it meant a lot of things. Listening to keep them safe. Listening to find them food. Listening for human activity. When she would stop, listen, and hold her breath, he knew she was worried. When she would stop and sniff, he knew she was trying to find them food. Silver learned early that when she held her breath, he needed to be absolutely still and do the same. He would wait for her to relax and then allow his body to soften again.

One fateful evening, while crossing a busy section of the interstate to try and find some more food, Silver disregarded his mother's warning. Andean, always cautious, beckoned her cub to follow her quickly across the road. But he became captivated by two bright lights coming his way. She looked back, expecting him right behind her but instead saw him standing in the road, staring into the headlights of an oncoming tractor trailer. She yelled out but it was too late. She watched, horrified and paralyzed, as his body was pulled over and under its tires. He was mangled right before her very eyes.

Andean ran over to him and felt her legs begin to give out under her as she stood over his lifeless body. More headlights were coming, and she felt as if she, too, had left her body, soaring into the sky to find her little boy. She watched herself run to the other side of the road and collapse with grief. She became aware of her body again and began frantically pacing and gasping for air that wouldn't fill her lungs. She was sure her heart would implode from the crushing weight of despair against her deflated chest. Not knowing what else to do, she began to run.

Andean's legs, numb and trembling, finally buckled beneath her, and she collapsed into a heap at the bottom of a ravine along the interstate. Morning arrived with the roar of passing cars above her. She could not shake the horrific vision of Silver being dragged under the tires of the truck. She wept inconsolably; her voice was mangled from calling out for hours. Clawing frantically at the dirt and grass below her, she showered herself with earth, trying to bury her grief and rage. Her bellows echoed in the forest, the trees stoically sharing her pain.

In the days that followed, Andean questioned if she had imagined Silver altogether. Nightmares plagued her, driving her to frantically start searching for him, thinking he had wandered off, only to confront the cruel truth of his absence. With no clear direction, she followed the road westward, skirting the edge of the forest. Andean had no desire to return to the alcove she and Silver had called home. For days, she continued on her journey, guided only by the distant hum of the traffic. Her sole desire - to escape the memory of Silver and the grief that consumed her.

Hunter

Hunter now spent his days testing Henry and Faith's powers of observation. With little else to occupy his time, he carefully manipulated their belongings, observing any changes in their behavior. Initially, he experimented by subtly rearranging items, like shifting picture frames or displacing plates, to gauge their reaction. Surprisingly, they sometimes acknowledged the alterations, but only for objects that had remained undisturbed for extended periods. However, their indifference remained steadfast when it came to everyday items like sandals or socks.

One day Hunter driven by both boredom and curiosity, Hunter decided to escalate his experiments. Seizing a set of keys, a familiar object he had already tampered with before, he boldly moved them to a different room. Displeased by their lack of response, he dropped the keys in the center of the living room, eyeing them intently. But he wasn't satisfied yet. Examining the keys closely, he noticed a distinctive black-handled one adorned with an unfamiliar symbol. Intrigued by their significance to the humans, he batted them around playfully before entertaining a mischievous idea.

With a flick of his paw, Hunter hoisted the keys, clamping one of the rings between his teeth. After a couple of clumsy attempts, he successfully carried them to his cat bed, a playful challenge to Henry and Faith's observational skills. As he awaited their return, a surge of anticipation washed over him, mingled with a hint of mischief. In the ensuing silence, he remained alert, eager to witness their reaction upon discovering the keys' disappearance.

Despite his excitement, he enjoyed a brief nap atop his cat bed where he waited, too anxious to move. He was jolted awake by the sound of keys outside of the door, which meant that Henry and Faith had returned from their outing. First, he heard Faith's voice, followed by Henry's bustling entrance, laden with plastic bags. Eagerly, Hunter bounded toward them, feigning excitement at their arrival. He yowled and paced around their feet, tail flicking nervously, casting furtive glances between their faces and the empty table where the keys once lay, the anticipation of their discovery weighing heavily in his stomach.

Yet, Henry and Faith remained engrossed in their conversation at the kitchen peninsula, oblivious to Hunter's antics. Undeterred, he continued his attempts to grab their attention, meowing and chirping incessantly. Eventually, Henry ambled over to Hunter's food bowl, depositing a scoop of kibble without his usual affectionate pat on the head. Henry's demeanor was solemn, tinged with irritation.

As the evening dragged on, he watched their every move as they kept themselves occupied with television, food, and more television. They barely talked all evening and seemed to be avoiding one another. Hunter found their silence disconcerting and started questioning his impulse to hide the keys. Finally, they went to bed and he was relieved; something about their interactions had him feeling uneasy. He lay in his bed in the dark and contemplated his next steps. He checked under his bed again to make sure the keys were still there and...yes! They were still there.

Contemplating how to return the keys unnoticed, Hunter weighed the risks of his plan. He dismissed the idea of moving them back to the table, fearing the inevitable noise would awaken Henry and Faith. Maneuvering the heavy keys back up to the tabletop seemed daunting. Despite his mounting anxiety, Hunter resolved to see his plan through.

It was two days later, after Hunter had contemplated how he would return the keys to the floor beneath the side table, that Henry's frantic search began. The missing keys resulted in an argument of epic proportions between Henry and Faith that Hunter could not have anticipated.

Beatrice

Beatrice remained locked in a gaze with the swan. Suddenly, the majestic bird twirled 180 degrees in a single swift motion, gliding across the lake without looking back, yet unmistakably aware of having captured the squirrel's attention. Mesmerized, Beatrice watched as the swan vanished around the bend, leaving ripples in the water, as if her spirit lingered behind.

Driven by an inexplicable force, Beatrice found herself darting across the grass and ascending the nearest tree. She yearned to draw closer to the pond and the enigmatic swan, the treetops offering her the best vantage point. Jumping from branch to branch, she navigated the bouncing limbs, her eyes fixed on the swan's rippling trail, fearing she might lose sight of it amidst the maze of foliage.

Finally, a gap in the leaves afforded Beatrice a clear view of the swan executing figure-eight motions along the pond's edge before vanishing beneath the drooping branches of a nearby willow. Determined, she descended the branch of the maple she traversed, nearly stumbling once but regaining her balance with her claws. With renewed resolve, she sprinted, launching herself towards the willow's rope-like branches.

She couldn't believe it: she made it! Beatrice was swaying back and forth on the leafy branch like a pendulum. Still jarred by the audacity of her courage, she waited for the branch to settle before slowly lowering herself to the damp, cool ground. She darted down the trunk of the tree and leaped towards the pond, springing around the perimeter of the tree towards the water. As she reached the water's edge her eyes scanned the water's surface in search of the swan's trail. Suddenly, out of the corner of her eye, she saw a flash of white: it was the swan, pacing just around the other side of the tree, awaiting the squirrel's arrival.

Beatrice stood for a moment, questioning whether she was imagining the connection she felt with the swan. *What could a swan want from her, a squirrel?* Of course, over the years in Boston she had seen plenty of swans in the park but had never interacted with any of them. She recalled witnessing the beautiful creatures having to aggressively fend off excited human tourists who were eager to get photos with the swans and in the process would get dangerously close to their tiny cygnets, following their mother in a neat row.

Gathering her courage, she charged towards the swan, unsure of her next move but trusting her intuition. As she approached, Beatrice found herself among three swans emerging from the other side of the tree. They stood regally before her, exuding warmth and dignity, their obsidian-black eyes meeting hers.

Almost instinctively, Beatrice lowered her head to them in reverence. They, too, nodded their heads in acknowledgement. The swan in the center lifted one wing to gesture towards some tall shrubbery just beyond the willow tree's branches, swaying in a blustery wind that seemed to come out of nowhere.

Deliberately, they all turned towards the cluster of bushes and began to walk towards it. She followed them.

Phillip

Phillip stood in the dimly illuminated hallway, his eyes adjusting to the darkness of this secret level. Dripping echoed in the distance, a slow patter of water on stone. The damp mustiness of the surroundings felt palpable, as though he were truly there.

Phillip had played his fair share of gory and creepy video games, stock-piled with jump scares and eerie vibes, a thrill he occasionally enjoyed when he needed a break from his preferred genre of action/adventure. This felt different though. He felt uneasy, staring down the dark, clammy catacomb tunnel: crumbling stone walls and ancient and brittle bones were stacked in recessed cubbies carved out of the wall structure. Compared to the softly focused lush greenery and textures of the settings of *Kingdom of Beasts*, this space felt as if it were created by a completely different developer.

The praying mantis, QueenOfHearts666, began jogging down the hall with purpose and speed. Still disoriented, Phillip followed suit but after a minute of trying to process the entire situation in his mind he decided he needed more answers.

"Hold up!" Phillip typed in the chat.

The green creature stopped and turned around. It dawned on Phillip that both of their costumes had changed as well. They now donned resplendent crimson velvet robes that were cinched around their centers with amber-gold tasseled ropes. Their robes did not have hoods but instead were accessorized with red and cold embroidered scarves draped around their shoulders.

Still awaiting a response from QueenOfHearts666, he typed more:

"What is this? Where are we?"

Jethro stood still, gently swaying from inaction, occasionally looking around his shoulders. QueenOfHearts666 did not move their avatar for an awkward amount of time, leading Phillip to believe that there was more to their story than just needing help getting through a challenging level.

Finally, they responded:

"You are not in the same game anymore…"

Confused, he replied as anyone might in his situation:

"What do you mean?"

While impatient for a reply he switched his attention to his phone and immediately Googled 'secret level kingdom of beasts.' The internet was full of gameplay secrets and cheat codes so he hoped he might find some answers online. As he scrolled down the first results page, then the second, and even into the third, he found nothing about catacombs.

Phillip watched the chat box eagerly awaiting their response. He put down his controller and brought his hands to cup his jaw in anticipation, nibbling at his hangnails and admonishing himself for doing so, all the while tapping his heel against the wheel of his gaming chair. Watching their avatar, still motionless, he wondered if they had walked away from the game altogether. He found himself picking at his hangnail again, but the ding of a chat notification pulled him out of his trance-like state back into reality. *Why was he so nervous?* His nervousness began to compound; as he questioned his nervousness, he just seemed to get more anxious. With sweaty palms, he picked up his controller and toggled to the chat box.

"This is a secret game, by invitation only. It has no name. Our players are selected by us, the developers. You have been chosen to join us."

The Crows

No crow has the same name as any other crow. Every crow, during maturation, chooses their own unique name in a spoken, not written, secret tongue; a highly intricate language shared with humans only once, hundreds of years ago, long before Columbus invaded the Americas.

Its complexity and vastness surpass that of any human language documented in Earth's history. The language of crows remained protected, with only a few chosen outside their species to wield the power of its enormity; it allowed them to experience life together, synchronically, through the many facets of their beautiful, celestial language. It had been kept a secret, of course, until the early 21st century following a series of massive ecological shifts at what would become known as "The Great Event" of the 21st century.

Crows can hear and comprehend with fluidity multitudes of human and non-human languages; they can interpret regional dialects within languages, can understand intonation and inflection, facial expressions, and body movement. Across centuries, they observed various means of communication among Earth's many species, and created their own unique, complicated, communication and mapping system, known only to them and used exclusively by them.

Crows are far more evolved than humans, their intellectual prowess having become embedded within their genetic code, allowing them to pass on their superior intellectual abilities to their spawn from generation to generation. They are born inherently with the self-awareness and intellectual capability of an adult human; their emotional intelligence, by adulthood, far surpasses that of any human adult.

From their perches in the treetops, they learned to use branches, dropped leaves, or small sticks to signal to other crows of human activity nearby. Shaking and pulling small twigs from dying trees they began arranging the fallen leaves and pinecones intentionally to create hidden messages for the others. In this way they could communicate with one another over long distances, leaving visual signs behind to deliver their messages further than their voices could carry.

This method allowed them to gain access to human territory without drawing attention to themselves, as humans rarely looked down or up, their eyes often fixated on their phones or the other humans around them. Their messages written with twigs, leaves, and litter remained invisible to the humans, oblivious to what was happening around them.

It is from the tops of trees that crows manage their affairs. They nest far into the deepest, dampest parts of the forests around the globe; their preference is evergreen trees wherein they can easily disappear. Crows will only make themselves visible to humans when necessary and reveal themselves only when searching for food; scavengers by nature but known to hunt mice and other small creatures, their food sources were quickly becoming scarce due to ongoing human interference in their complex, sustainable ecosystem.

To crows, humans were the most dangerous species on Earth.

Hunter

The hidden keys under Hunter's bed had initiated an explosive fight between Henry and Faith. Hunter had not anticipated the power this random object wielded over these humans; for something so small and seemingly insignificant to be the cause of such harbored rage made him all the more wary of his human 'companions.' To experience such a dramatic shift in their moods caused by something so seemingly irrelevant made him more fearful of them than ever.

A sudden urge to flee the house overwhelmed Hunter, affirming his lingering suspicion that these humans were not to be trusted.

Hunter was lounging in his bed when he heard Henry's long-awaited, "Have you seen my keys?" in an aggressive tone that made the hair on the back of Hunter's neck stand on end. Hunter immediately perked up, ready to observe, and even contemplated moving the keys to another room completely, such as the bathroom away from his bed; someplace obscure enough so as not to appear culpable. He changed his mind, however, as the situation began to escalate rapidly.

Taking refuge under the sofa, Hunter listened to the escalating argument, bewildered by the intensity over ordinary keys. Amidst shouting matches and accusatory gestures, he observed their faces flush with anger, their voices escalating until Henry stormed out, leaving Faith in tears.

Hunter lost any sense of time as he crouched frozen under the couch, hiding still even after Henry stormed out of the house, slamming the door behind him without looking back. Faith burst into tears then called someone on her phone. Hunter remained under there, eventually allowing the muscles in his neck and shoulders to relax but still no less alert.

He could hear Faith's voice in the other room, crying to the person on the other end. After some time in the bathroom, Faith finally emerged, still on the phone, clearly upset but no longer crying. She quickly put on her jacket, grabbed her purse, then left. It took some time, but Hunter was finally able to calm himself enough to use his paw to drag the keys out from underneath his bed. He stared down at the keys in fearful awe, unable to comprehend their importance.

Hunter began to replay the incident in his head over and over again. By the climax of their fight they were taking turns screaming, interrupting the other, and throwing items around in disgust at one another. The anger they projected did not feel natural to him no matter how many times he tried to justify their behavior.

In fact, it felt so unnatural that, after much pacing around and moving the keys from one location or another so as not to rouse suspicion, he finally decided to bat them under the couch.

He began planning his escape.

Sally

Sally sniffed at her food arranged purposefully in front of the closet. April's assistant had left almost as quickly as he had come, but Sally made sure to stand over her kibble so that he wouldn't step on the arrangement. She studied it for quite some time, all the while selling that another animal had been in her room. She nosed a couple of the pieces but made sure to put them back in place, trying to make sense of why someone would want to leave her food in this pattern and, even more perplexing, not eat it, as most creatures would.

While living in Manhattan, Sally had her fair share of encounters with mice, rats, and occasionally cockroaches. From what she remembered, this smell mostly reminded her of the mice that would occasionally make their way into April's kitchen, prompting a visit from a maintenance worker who would set up traps for them. He was a friendly man; he stopped in from time to time to fix leaky faucets or to replace a smoke detector, and always carried dog treats with him.

"In my line of work," he would say to April, "I need to make friends with the animal tenants -occupational hazard, you know?" His voice was always warm and his presence soothing.

The comforting memory made Sally miss her home in Manhattan. Now she was stuck, alone and bored in this bleak hotel room, and could not stop obsessing over the circle of kibble left by some rodent in their hallway. She finally decided to leave it and wait for April's reaction when she saw the unusual display. The assistant had been too busy with his phone to look down and notice. Humans rarely looked down these days, she mused, or even up. They were all staring at their phones.

When April came back to the hotel, she walked right past the kibble display and, to Sally's dismay, her as well. She was, of course, talking on her phone, obviously excited about the success of her book, to a friend whose voice Sally recognized. April barely looked down at Sally who was dancing wildly around her feet trying to get her attention.

Later, as April prepared Sally's meal, Sally ensured there would be leftovers to respond to the mysterious stranger's gesture. However, April quickly cleared away the food, wary of attracting pests common in such places. Sally knew she'd have to hide some food before April removed her dish and put it in the sink.

It sometimes irritated Sally how quickly April would assume she was done eating simply because she had stepped away from her dish. Sometimes she needed to give her stomach time to digest but would soon grow hungry again after the food was removed. Sally occasionally would overeat, fearful that she would not have enough to keep her content through the night, and then she would feel sick and miserable for the rest of the evening.

April was in the hotel kitchen, nose in her phone, simultaneously preparing Sally's dinner while scrolling on Instagram. Sally looked on, April's thumb appearing a blur as it rapidly tapped photos and flicked through stories on her screen. She would occasionally check on the steamed sweet potatoes and sweet peas, poking them with a fork, followed by her ritual of opening the oven, inserting a thermometer into the roasting bird, and closing the oven again, dissatisfied by its progress. April's phone rang and she walked out on the balcony to take the call. Sally grew irritated, hungry and left alone with the smell of baked chicken and veggies in the air, but no way to access it.

After what seemed like an eternity, April returned from the balcony, still blabbing away with someone on the other end about her next book gig, a signing event where Sally would likely be toted along for photo ops. She headed to the kitchen and grabbed a kitchen towel to pull the roasted chicken out of the oven. Sally's stomach growled furiously as she watched April carve two small pieces from the breast of the chicken, her phone now on speaker as she used a fork to gently place the chicken on a plate along with several pieces of sweet potato. Grabbing a spoon, she began to dish out some of the peas as well.

The food was left steaming on a plate up on the counter. April walked away, gesturing in annoyance while she instructed the voice on the other end.

"As I said, I need to be assured that Sally won't be handled by any children during the signing. She gets anxious around small children, and she is *not* some emotional support service dog."

Sally, rather indifferent towards children, was furious with April as she watched her food steaming above her in the kitchen. Not only was she starving, but she was also eager to leave her visitor a message to let them know she was a friend. She would somehow use her dinner to leave them a sign. Sally paced around the kitchen, whimpering pathetically in hopes that April would take notice of her.

Finally, April hurried out of the bedroom, grabbed Sally's dinner from the counter and placed it on the floor in the hallway. She hadn't even acknowledged Sally as she normally would, with a reassuring head pat or by hyping her up for the dinner she had prepared. April quickly walked away, pressing the buttons on her phone to call her assistant with the itinerary for the next day.

While April was distracted on the phone, Sally took the opportunity to mouth a few pieces of potato and peas and place them carefully and strategically between the fridge and the wall, hopeful that April wouldn't take notice of the food. She then picked at the chicken and potatoes (not a big fan of peas), until she felt satiated. Her excitement about leaving a message for her visitor, left a fluttery, leaping feeling in her stomach that took away much of her appetite.

April fell silent, still in the bedroom, and Sally waited impatiently, hovering in the hallway between the kitchen and bedroom. Finally, she heard the sound she had been waiting for: the shower being turned on and the bathroom door closing. This was her moment!

Racing to the kitchen where she left the potatoes and peas, Sally grabbed them gently between her front teeth and moved them one by one to the front door. In the dim light from the hallway, she arranged them in a circle, convinced it would catch the visitor's attention. Stepping back, she admired her handiwork, hoping April wouldn't stumble upon the scraps.

Now she just hoped that April wouldn't venture into the entryway and find the food scraps. So as not to draw attention to it, Sally made her way back into the bedroom and into her little bed, next to April's. She lay waiting, listening to the sound of the shower water slapping against the side of the glass shower wall as April rinsed her hair, a familiar and comforting sound. She began to feel drowsy and fought sleep, startling at every creaking noise she heard in the distance, wondering if her visitor was out there at that very moment.

She must have eventually drifted off to sleep because she was startled awake as April shuffled in from the bathroom, steam rolling out behind her, and moved towards the dresser to grab her pajamas. Relieved, she watched April dress herself for bed and slip under the blankets, phone in hand as usual. April didn't acknowledge Sally lying beside her below as she turned to shut off the lamp on her nightstand. Click. The light turned off and the ceiling flickered with blue light from her phone. April's face looked eerily intense as she scrolled through her social media pages.

As Sally slipped back into sleep, she was haunted by strange dreams of chasing shadows and mysterious noises throughout the hotel room.

Andean

Andean had lost count of the days she'd spent traveling westward alongside the interstate. Each morning, she rose with the sun, driven by an aimless urge to flee westward, away from the tormenting warmth and beauty of the sun, away from the painful absence of Silver. She resented the daylight that illuminated the aged bark of tree trunks, a cruel reminder of Silver's soft fur.

In the gnarled stumps and roots of rotting trees, Andean saw echoes of Silver's stoic face, his soft eyes that once filled her heart with joy. But joy was fleeting, replaced by a relentless ache that felt like glass tearing at her insides. She was bewildered by the warm tears that stained her fur, leaving permanent marks of her grief.

The sun beamed through the rustling leaves and pine needles of the forest ceiling, casting moving shadows all around her. Andean feared the flickering shadows dancing around her and kept her head down as low as possible to avoid their cruel deceptions. At times she was certain she could see Silver's round rump bobbing up and down around and amongst the chervil and birch trees, or his perky black ears ducking under some nearby ferns. When she first saw these illusions, Andean would dash to investigate the shadows, frantically sniffing through the green foliage and questioning whether perhaps she had only dreamed Silver's death and was now waking from a horrible nightmare; surely, she would find him curled up in a ball waiting for her in some quiet hollow. But she never found him.

One early morning, as she continued on her somber sojourn, Andean suddenly emerged from the woods into a field surrounded by a metal fence where she found herself face-to-face with a herd of cattle, who were grazing and looking up at her with unbothered curiosity. Some continued to stare but most quickly lost interest, lowering their heads and continuing to graze on the grass around them. Andean found solace in their presence and decided to rest awhile, locking her eyes on one particular butterscotch colored cow.

The cow stood motionless; her gaze fixed on Andean until the bear's tense muscles eased. With a deep, imploring bleat, she signaled to the others to move away from this side of the meadow. Andean watched as the rest of the herd rolled away calmly, as if silently saying; almost as if to say, *please, just leave us be.*

As they ambled away, the bear watched their low-hanging udders, swollen with milk, yet marred by scars and weathered by time. Andean was reminded of her little Silver and the sharp pains she endured during his early suckling days. His jaw and tongue worked frantically and furiously to draw her milk into his throat, desperate to fill his empty belly. It did not take long, however, for him to learn that he needed to drink her milk gently. When his suckling became too aggressive, she would resort to swatting and biting him, sometimes growling, to let him know he was hurting her. Seeing the cows' battered nipples filled her with dread, wondering where their calves were, to leave their udders so full.

A sense of foreboding gnawed at Andean as she sensed something amiss in the cows' demeanor. Their slow, purposeless gait spoke of mourning, of defeat. Andean watched as they descended towards the valley, tails swinging slowly in retreat. A shroud of sadness enveloped her, reigniting her own grief. She longed to join them, finding solace in shared sorrow.

Reverently, Andean walked back into the forest so as not to disturb or distress them anymore. Her experience with the cows gave her a feeling of belonging; she was comforted somehow knowing that she was not alone in her suffering, and it gave her a new sense of purpose, though she was not quite sure what that purpose might be. She also became aware of her own freedom after seeing the cows with their ears tagged with numbers and realized that she had happened upon a prison of sorts. She found a spot in the woods not far from the field where she made herself a nest to rest in and reflect and decided she would stay here for a while and observe her bovine sisters. Not long after settling into her new home, Andean felt a familiar sensation in her stomach that surprised her: a craving for fresh berries.

Since Silver's death she had not desired any food and was barely aware of the flavors of the food she did manage to forage during her travels. The pleasure of food had escaped her, as it reminded her keenly of Silver's joy when he would spot blackberry bushes, running from her side to gorge himself on them until he became so full that he would need to nap. She loved watching his eyes twitch and flutter, his mouth in a half smile, as he lay curled up next to her. Sometimes his paws would move as if he was dreaming about picking berries, or maybe chasing butterflies, another favorite playtime activity of his.

She could almost taste the sweet tartness of blackberries on her tongue just from reminiscing about her baby. Almost frantically, Andean sprang up and began to forage, desperate to feel the juicy crunch of berries in her mouth. Her senses started to come alive again as she sniffed around the forest foliage. In her search she happened upon a beehive and could smell the sweet honey wafting from inside; elation overwhelmed her as she could feel Silver's excitement pulling at her from deep within her soul, an energy that seemed to radiate from her sternum.

Driven by reminiscence, Andean sprang into action, foraging eagerly. She stumbled upon a beehive, the scent of honey stirring memories of Silver's delight. With renewed vigor, she approached the hive, recalling the stings endured for his sake. Climbing the tree, she seized the honeycomb, welcoming both pain and pleasure. She could feel herself coming alive again: the sweetness of the honey coating her tongue and cheeks, the sugary crunch of the comb as she chomped down on it.

Savoring the honeycomb, tears flowed freely, mingling with the sticky sweetness. In this bittersweet moment, Andean felt her spirit stir, Silver's essence intertwined with hers. Exhausted but revived, she succumbed to sleep beneath the pine, the gentle hum of bees lulling her into a peaceful slumber.

Phillip

Phillip now stood in front of his screen, controller clutched in his hands, a flood of questions swirling in his mind. Before he could articulate them, a message materialized:

"Okay, I have to leave but you are free to explore as much as you want. We will meet again."

The avatar vanished, leaving Phillip alone in the catacomb hallway. What was his mission? Did he even have one? He checked his inventory, surprised to find it intact, brimming with weapons and supplies.

The graphics used in the design of his weaponry, much like his surroundings, had changed from the original game. All of it was obviously made by a completely different developer. Phillip looked around to assess his surroundings using the 360-zoom feature. From what he could tell, he had only two directions to go: forward or backward. Although the secret entrance had been through the catacomb wall, there was no obvious exit or entrance to either his left or right.

Phillip started forward, walking and then jogging past dimly lit dirt walls adorned with human skulls and bones, arranged along inlets carved into the walls. There was no sound but his footsteps and distant water dripping, he felt his heart racing in anticipation of a jump scare or attack. But after a few minutes on high alert, he encountered nothing new: no rooms or doors, just a long hallway that seemed to go on forever. He glanced at the clock. It was 2:12 a.m. Jerked back into reality, Phillip realized he had to be up in just a few hours to teach middle-schoolers.

Contemplating shutting down, he hesitated, fearing he might not regain access to this hidden level. Googling again yielded nothing. Putting down his controller he went to his refrigerator for a drink. Orange juice, water, milk, or … yes! - Red Bull!

Phillip mentally reviewed the next day's course plans for his students. Animal kingdoms and classification were next up in his curriculum. This was only the second year he had been teaching it, as one of the junior-most teachers on staff. Maybe he could pull up some reruns of *Bill Nye the Science Guy* on YouTube and let Bill tackle the animal kingdoms. He assured himself that every teacher has resorted to videos battling sleep deprivation, himself included, but there were only three weeks before mid-terms. Losing a day could be a setback for some of his more challenged students.

Phillip's conscience kept him hovering in front of the refrigerator, holding the door open and stalling his decision between water and Red Bull. He closed the fridge and went back to his gaming area, his avatar still bobbing in place. He recalled more than a few all-nighters back in college, fueled by Diet Coke and gummy bears, scrambling to complete a big paper or cramming for an exam.

His mind made up, Phillip returned to the fridge and grabbed the Red Bull, trying to harness the same can-do-20-year-old energy to pull off his lesson on next to no sleep. He was determined to find somewhere in this game where he could save his progress. He was irritated with himself for not asking QueenOfHearts666 about it. *Would he lose access if he logged off? Did he have to advance to a new level before he could save his progress?*

Sitting back down at his desk, he guzzled the Red Bull and pulled a bag of pretzels from a nearby drawer. After shoving a few in his mouth, he grabbed his controller, got comfortable in his chair with the bag of pretzels tucked between his thighs, and forged ahead. After another ten minutes of jogging and exploring the same seemingly endless tunnel, Phillip grew discouraged.

Instead of calling it quits, Phillip decided to try a different approach. He would allow Jethro to advance a few feet and then inspect each new section of wall, zooming in and out, pressing the button for grabbing objects and jumping up to see if there was another secret portal he could access.

2:56 a.m.

Phillip's eyes were growing tired and dry, and he was ready to call it quits and head to bed, hoping that if he left his system running, he could just return to it the next day when he got home from work. Phillip toggled to change the perspective to first-person and instantly noticed markings on the ground that hadn't been visible before. At first, he thought they might be water marks or shadows, but as he inspected them more closely, he discovered that they seemed to create a pattern. No, they weren't random at all. They were symbols! They weren't like hieroglyphics or names carved with tools; the symbols had been crafted using water. What was more perplexing was that the water marks looked fresh, as if spilled onto the ground intentionally to make the design: a triangle with a circle in the center and three matching circles flanking each side of the triangle.

Phillip maneuvered Jethro to hover over the symbol and, immediately, a hidden door materialized, revealing a bone-lined tunnel. With newfound energy, Phillip guided Jethro through, fearing the passage might seal shut behind them. As they passed through, the door slammed shut, sealing their fate.

There was no going back.

Hunter

Hunter had been strategizing his escape since the explosive confrontation between Henry and Faith over the missing keys a week ago. Aware that his best chance lay in fleeing through the front door, he knew timing was crucial. Venturing outside before had only led to indecision and capture, so he needed a plan.

He had to be more calculated and act while they were distracted, perhaps when they returned from one of their outings and, even better, when their arms were full of bags or packages when they did. Hunter started to track the times they would typically come home with their hands full of grocery bags. He assessed their ritual of leaving and coming back with food, tracking the days and nights in between, and calculated that they would leave and come back with groceries every five to seven days.

Hunter spent his days now surveying the neighborhood from his favorite window perch, deciding on the best possible escape route with the most opportunity to hide from Henry and Faith's view. The wooded area behind the house seemed to offer the best opportunity. He moved from window to window in each room to assess his escape route and practice it in his mind. The window ledges were narrow with not much space for his fifteen-pound girth to find purchase, but he was determined to uncover the mysteries beyond the outer walls of this house. He practiced jumping up on the sills, often falling back down as he lost his balance on the precarious ledges and occasionally knocking down the clutter they stored there. Faith, of course, was greatly annoyed when she came home to find her precious odds and ends on the floor below.

"What has gotten into you?" she would reprimand him.

With determination, Hunter mastered the art of graceful movement, navigating the cluttered sills with precision: jumping up onto the backs of chairs without using his claws, catching his balance, and walking slowly and carefully, one paw in front of the other, as if walking on a tightrope. He became more conscious of his body: aware of the pooch drooping from his stomach, he would arch his back to lift the low-hanging fur as he walked in and among their trinkets. In the span of a week, he had mastered jumping up, holding himself still, and navigating around the frames and baubles on the windowsills.

From their bedroom window, he studied the backyard, eyeing the cypress shrubs and wooden fence. Could he scale it? Uncertain of his physical prowess after years of inactivity, Hunter pondered his escape route, aware that his freedom hinged on his ability to navigate the obstacles ahead.

Hunter practiced his climbing skills by using the upholstered furniture to determine whether his forelegs were strong enough to pull himself up vertically. This also got him into trouble, as his claws left scratch marks on the furniture and sent Faith into another fit of rage but, this time, she took it out on Henry which caused yet another spat between the two of them.

"I'm always the one cleaning his litter, dealing with his messes, and making sure he gets vet appointments. Feeding him! Doing dishes! Doing laundry!"

The quarrel went back and forth, and Hunter hid under the couch and tried to ignore them, until something Faith said caught his attention and sent chills down his spine:

"We need to get him declawed – he is an indoor cat, what does he even need claws for anyways?" Faith retorted.

Hunter, like most cats, could understand human language clearly, so he knew exactly what this meant. Henry was opposed, citing abuse and articles he had read about the procedure and its impact on cats. Faith turned it around, claiming that she wished Henry would put the same amount of thought into her and her needs.

Yup, Hunter had to get out. And soon!

He decided that the next time he saw one of them come into the driveway he would be ready by the door to make his escape.

Cadillac

Cadillac had lost track of the time that had passed but was pretty sure she had been wandering in the forest for at least three days at this point. Her grief had suppressed her appetite, but she was starting to feel weak from not eating and barely resting. Fearful of being found and brought back to the shelter, she didn't dare leave the woods.

At one point she heard voices and hid crouched down among some ferns as hikers passed by along a nearby trail. Realizing she was too close to the human trails, Cadillac sought refuge deeper into the forest, climbing higher to avoid detection. Her once pristine, fluffy gray fur was now muddied and matted; mosquitos and black flies were relentlessly attacking her, mostly around her eyes and nose where her protective coat was sparse.

At last, around sunset, Cadillac found a stream that she was able to bathe herself in. Its frigid water brought her great relief and soothed the painful, itchy welts from her many insect bites. She lay down in the stream and let the icy water flow over her, numbing her sore muscles and tattered paws. She felt defeated and unsure of what to do next. When she realized she couldn't feel her toes anymore, she knew it was time to get out of the water. She managed to crawl out of the rocky stream and collapsed onto the mossy shore. As she raised her head, she saw an alcove under a nearby rock formation and cautiously headed towards it. Her paws were raw and tender, and she winced in pain with each step, finally coming to a stop under its shelter. She circled in the bracken to make a bed for herself in the alcove. Exhausted, she fell into a deep, deep sleep.

Suddenly, she was awakened by a gentle nudge on her flank. Opening her eyes, she was met by the sight of a large, gray and brown wolf, its intense yellow eyes fixed upon her but devoid of aggression. Three more wolves stood behind him, their presence imposing yet strangely serene. Trembling with fear, Cadillac recognized her vulnerability, resigned to her fate as she lowered her head with a whimper, accepting whatever lay ahead.

To her surprise, the large brown and black wolf took several steps back as the jet-black wolf emerged from behind him, dropping from her jowls a rabbit, limp and lifeless, on the ground in front of the despondent dog. Cadillac herself had never hunted, other than pouncing on rodents playfully in Roland's backyard.

Sensing her hesitation, the wolves exchanged glances, and the black and brown wolf approached her, his tail lifted in a sign of friendship. Lowering his head to the carcass, he tore it open with his teeth, starting at the neck and revealing the tender meat underneath. After taking a small bite for himself, he nudged the carcass toward her and sat down.

Timid and shaky, Cadillac approached the rabbit, inhaling its unfamiliar aroma. Still warm, it beckoned to her primal instincts. As she gnawed at the flesh, its tangy and savory flavor awakened her senses, igniting a rush of carnal energy. Overwhelmed by her newfound ferocity, she devoured the meat, using her paws to tear away more and more.

Returning to her senses, she realized she had consumed most of the rabbit. Fearful of upsetting the wolves with her gluttony, she looked up to find them calmly grooming each other, indifferent to her carnivorous display. They rested at the mouth of the cave, their attention focused outward, unperturbed by her actions.

Sam

Quite some time had passed since Sam's encounter with the gray dog, yet the experience changed him. He couldn't pinpoint the exact change within himself, but he felt a growing unease that hadn't been there before. Before the dog's escape, his days blended together seamlessly. His routine rarely varied: awaken, forage, rest, forage again, and finally return to his tunneled home at sunset. He never ventured far from his burrows.

Sam took great pride in his burrow, a testament to his architectural prowess. It comprised several tunnels leading to his main sleeping chamber, a second chamber reserved for a potential mate (groundhogs prefer their own space), and a designated bathroom chamber. At the heart of it all lay a turnaround chamber, allowing navigation between the tunnels while maintaining security against predators and preventing collapses. Despite his stout frame, he proved quite the contortionist.

That night, after aiding the dog, Sam slept fitfully, plagued by strange dreams that lingered long after waking. In one he found himself lost in his own tunnels, hearing cries for help echoing around him but unable to find the chamber from whence the sounds were coming. In one, he found himself lost in his own tunnels, the cries of an unseen creature echoing around him. Desperate to locate the source, he dug furiously, only to feel the cries slipping further away, as if retreating into the dirt walls themselves. Each awakening left him frustrated and haunted.

During Sam's foraging walks he found himself stopping to look behind him more frequently than usual, haunted by a strange feeling that he was being watched. His eyes caught small movements in the grass that he had been oblivious to before. He noticed movements in the grass he once ignored: insects hopping from leaf to leaf, wind gusts shifting branches, chipmunks each other through the underbrush, and field mice scurrying beneath the foliage. But why, now, did he feel as if their eyes were constantly upon him?

Sam had this feeling that at any moment something was going to jump out of the brush toward him, which had made his usually enjoyable foraging rambles considerably less so; there was some kind of energy in the air that was forewarning him of events yet to come. These premonitions frightened Sam, who began to spend more and more time in his resting chamber and less and less time above ground. He knew he should be preparing for his winter hibernation, but his anxiety was getting the best of him.

Foraging had become more strategic and tactical: Sam found focal points in the woods to track his wanderings, relying less on smell as he had in the past and more on his vision. Without realizing it, he had become aware of time and its passing (loosely) as he would count his steps or breaths to track the amount of time it took to move from behind one stump to another, scanning for tall foliage or rocks to hide behind in case of emergencies. No longer motivated by the amount of food he could find in a day, his days were measured instead in time spent running and hiding, making each day feel progressively longer than the one before.

With this strange heightening of his senses, Sam noticed what he could only describe as bizarre coincidences during his foraging trips. While sniffing and digging in the underbrush, he might happen upon a pile of neatly arranged pinecones placed atop a mossy patch or, during one of his most recent outings, stacked in a pile on top of an old tree stump, one acorn placed in perfect balance at the very top. He tried to shake these findings, telling himself it was a playful bear cub. He had rarely seen humans this deep into the forest, but it could be possible they were the culprits. Yet broken branches arranged like ornaments in the trees unnerved him, swaying ominously in the wind.

Late autumn brought a chill to the air, the first mild frost leaving Sam shivering. He realized he hadn't fattened enough for winter's harshness. Panic gripped him as food grew scarcer, contemplating risky forays into human gardens. With mornings growing colder and daylight waning, Sam felt compelled to return to the house where he met the gray dog. Memories of its bountiful gardens offered a glimmer of hope.

The following morning, stomach churning but his resolve firm, Sam embarked on his journey back to the house, determined to survive the impending winter.

Beatrice

Standing before the massive shrubs by the willow tree with the swans, Beatrice puzzled over how they would navigate the dense growth. The swans, towering over her, elegantly maneuvered through a small opening at the base of the hedge. The last swan glanced back, urging her to follow, then vanished, ghostlike, into the foliage. The nimble squirrel squeezed through the narrow branchy entrance, fixating on the swan's tail feathers before they disappeared completely from view.

Cautiously, Beatrice made her way through the brambles of the shrub's undergrowth. Sunlight filtered through the leaves overhead, casting an orange glow over a long tunnel ahead. Its branches had been intentionally moved aside, clearing a path large enough to walk through with ease. Emerging into a clearing flanked by dense scrubs, she spotted the swans ahead, ducking under a large hydrangea bush that marked the end of the shrubbery walls.

Only hesitating for a moment, she darted underneath the hydrangea foliage and found herself in a clearing at its base. Among the swans stood a raccoon, several rats, three cats, a turtle, and four doves. Approaching them apprehensively, Beatrice lowered her tail and sat on her hind legs, uncertain of what to do next. A tense silence enveloped them as they observed each other, all sensing the unusual gathering. She wasn't the only newcomer; she could tell by the body language of some of the others.

Beatrice waited, hoping for some form of unspoken answer to her unformed question, unsure of exactly what that question should be other than, *what are we doing here?* With great care and finesse, the raccoon turned around to grab something from behind her. Dragging it along the ground to the middle of the group, she revealed a phone clutched between her fingers, and set it on the ground before the group. Hovering over the phone, she tapped on the screen, and it illuminated the inside of the natural tent with its bluish light.

The doves drew nearer, followed by the others. The swans, though, remained still, their long necks sweeping over the smaller creatures, bringing their faces closer to the screen. The raccoon tapped the screen repeatedly, then shifted it to the side of the clearing, propping it against a nearby branch. As they gathered around, Beatrice watched in horror as the footage unfolded: animals confined in cages, tubes attached in laboratories, and cruel beatings and slaughters. The scenes churned her stomach, yet she couldn't tear her gaze away.

Beatrice began to feel dizzy but couldn't avert her eyes. She realized that the somber music that she heard was also emanating from the small device, amplifying the sorrow and anger she felt growing inside; to see such acts of violence for no apparent reason made her feel sick to her stomach. She looked up and around at the others and could tell which critters had already seen the footage and which hadn't: they were watching the new-comers intently, gauging their reactions, the shock faded and became shrouded in cold fury. Beatrice had always known humans to be careless and unaffected by their acts of cruelty, but this video revealed them to bc truly barbaric.

When the video stopped, another one started playing. Then another. And another. Finally, the raccoon tapped the screen to stop the horrors. The swan nearest to Beatrice gave the raccoon a subtle nod, a cue to signal the raccoon to play another video. Beatrice wasn't sure how the raccoon knew how to operate this phone, but she tapped carefully again into the phone and a new video appeared. This time it was a video of humans. But they were not like the humans she saw walking around Boston: they were wearing very different clothing, some wearing long fabric garb that flowed down to their ankles, some wearing fine-looking suits with tall hats and pocket watches. There were no cars, only horses either carrying humans on their backs or tied to carriages with humans in them.

They were talking to each other, but not the way that she had heard humans speak to each other in the city; they spoke in sing-song voices, like birds, and moved synchronically. It reminded her of watching flocks of birds flying in the sky, moving in unison to create moving pictures in the sky. The hydrangea bush was filled with orchestral music, voices blending in harmony and making such beautiful sounds that it touched Beatrice in a way she had never felt; she was brought back to the tragedies of her lost friends and family listening to the passion with which they sang and danced. Their faces carried so many emotions: joy, sadness, anger, and fear. She didn't need to understand their language to understand how they felt: they were also enraged.

They remained captivated by the videos until Beatrice noticed the fading light within the shrub. Nightfall was approaching, and Beatrice grew anxious about returning home safely. Yet, she couldn't tear herself away from the captivating scenes. As if anticipating her thoughts, the raccoon turned off the phone and returned it to its hiding place. The swan, whom Beatrice now recognized as the leader, gestured towards the exit of their hideaway, and the others followed suit, each departing in their own direction.

Seeing the orange glow of sunset, Beatrice sprinted towards her nest. She felt a sense of being summoned back to the hydrangea bush the next day, as if she were now part of an undisclosed plot.

Returning home safely, Beatrice lay awake, reflecting on the day's events and the revelations from the phone. Eventually, she drifted into sleep, only to find herself in a dream. The room was filled with green walls and metal cages, yet they were all empty despite the echoing chittering and shrieks. Lost in the maze of hallways, Beatrice searched desperately for an exit, each turn leading her to yet another hallway filled with empty cages.

Hunter

Hunter spent his days meticulously preparing for his escape, honing his climbing, jumping, and balancing skills. Each movement was calculated, every route memorized to perfection. At night, he practiced his agility, darting gracefully from room to room, careful not to disturb the household debris that cluttered the floors. Faith's irritation with his nocturnal activities was palpable, her outbursts disrupting the household peace and leading to further tension between her and Henry.

At night he practiced dashing back and forth from room to room, navigating from one to the next swiftly and gracefully so as not to run into any obstacles or trip on the inevitable floor debris left by his owners. He was not completely silent however, which, of course, irritated Faith immensely; she would charge in from their bedroom yelling at him to stop. Her tirade would wake Henry and that would turn the provocation into yet another fight.

The anticipated moment finally arrived when Henry planned an evening out, leaving Faith to handle the grocery shopping alone. Hunter seized the opportunity, knowing Faith would be preoccupied with bags upon her return. As evening approached, he stationed himself on a narrow sill, overlooking the front of the house, where the parked cars lined the curb. An accidental disturbance with a succulent pot left Hunter unfazed, his focus solely on the impending escape.

Time dragged on but the butterflies in his stomach persisted. Hunter was just now realizing that he had spent all this time planning his escape but hadn't thought about his survival once free: food, water, a place to sleep. He began to doubt the wisdom of his intentions. He reminded himself repeatedly of all the reasons he would be better off on his own. Maybe he could live many, many more years in this house, with them taking care of his basic needs. *But was it worth it? To live longer, but under such stressful conditions?*

Lost in thought, he was jolted by the sight of Faith's car pulling up to the curb. His heart began to race, and he found himself running to the door, to the very spot he had picked out to hide. Beneath a small bench, tucked away among mittens and hats, he crouched, holding his breath as Faith's footsteps drew nearer. The rustle of bags and the click of keys signaled her arrival, heightening Hunter's tension.

The door opened and as Faith bent to retrieve the bags, Hunter seized his opportunity. Darting between her legs, he navigated the corners of the house with practiced agility, making a mad dash to the backyard. Leaping onto the fence, he felt a sharp sting as he landed on twigs on the other side. Ignoring the pain, he pressed on, slipping into the cover of trees and bushes, his instinct driving him forward.

Finally, in the safety of the shrubbery he inspected his would and found he had to pull a small twig from his side. He licked at it to soothe the pain but only for a moment, remembering that Faith may be looking for him. He fought his way through some ferns and underbrush before finding himself on another street lined with houses.

Hunter ducked back into the trees and bushes that were separating the streets and, without thinking, kept running, staying in the wooded stretch so as to avoid any humans. The sun was setting, and the shadows cast along the houses provided Hunter with more camouflage. He had hoped he would feel more comfortable sneaking around at night, with less chance of being spotted, but he began to feel more afraid as it got darker. He felt vulnerable and unsafe. He decided it would be best to find a spot to take cover in until daylight.

Andean

Andean woke up, slowly, as if she had been asleep for years. Disoriented, she started to remember her experience with the cows. The memory of their sorrow shook her, snapping her back into life. She opened her eyes and, adjusting to the sunlight, took in the scenery around her. The colors in the forest appeared more vibrant than they had the day before. She felt reconnected to the Earth, no longer a ghost wandering around without purpose. She felt compelled to go back to the farm, to see the cows again so they would know she hadn't forgotten them.

With renewed determination, Andean navigated her way back to the pasture using her heightened sense of smell. Scaling the metal fence proved challenging, but with persistence, she managed to hoist herself over, blending into the tall grass and shrubs along the perimeter.

Disappointment clouded her as she found the field empty, loneliness creeping back in. Yet, undeterred, she pressed on, tracing the tree line toward the distant red barn, flanked by towering silos. There, she spotted the herd basking in the morning sun, their breath visible in the crisp air. Human figures bustled about, tending to the feeding cages, making it impossible for Andean to draw nearer without detection.

Her gaze drifted to a nearby building, its aluminum structure casting a foreboding shadow. Inside, cows stood motionless, their solemn demeanor unsettling. Andean couldn't shake the feeling of impending doom, sensing a silent agony that mirrored her own. As she watched, she felt the weight of a terrible secret, buried within the depths of their sorrowful eyes, echoing with each graze and restless movement.

Andean nestled among the nearby ferns and pine trees, observing the farm for an extended period. She watched as cows were ushered into the building, only to emerge later and rejoin the grazing herd outside. Contemplating whether to visit during the night, when the humans were absent, she felt a familiar pang of hunger gnawing at her stomach. Retreating into the woods, she sought out a rotting log, a treasure trove of grubs, worms, and insects to satiate her appetite. Delighted by her discovery, she feasted on the bounty before deciding to move closer to the farm, avoiding the darkness of the woods.

When it was completely dark, she was able to see lights coming from a house not far from the barns and decided it was time to do some sleuthing. Mindful of every step and fearful of the sound of branches snapping under her feet, she treaded lightly down towards the building, which was still lit by fluorescent lights, allowing her to see inside. There were moths and other flying insects fluttering around the ceiling near the lights hanging above. Underneath the swarming bugs she saw humans, sweeping aisles surrounded by metal bars and strange metallic equipment. They were moving up and down through the aisles sweeping dirt. Dust swirled from their brooms, creating large brown clouds that wafted around their work boots as they moved about.

Nearby, the big red barn stood dimly lit, its surroundings shrouded in darkness. Andean surveyed the area meticulously, her eyes attuned to the night. Following a worn path in the grass, she approached the barn, eventually reaching a ramp leading to two large, bolted doors. Circling around, she stood on her hind legs to peer through a window, only to be met by the gaze of a large heifer. Startled but undeterred, Andean composed herself and rose again, meeting the cow's gaze, finding it unalarmed and unperturbed.

The cow's eyes were kind and sincere and she slowly backed away from the window, lowering herself onto a large pile of hay near the cell wall. Laying down, her udder spilled out from underneath her legs and belly onto the hay. Andean could feel the cow's exhaustion, could sense the pain in her legs and hips from standing all day, her sore udder, and an overall sense of fatigue and hopelessness. She felt tears welling in her eyes again. The cow let out a soft mooing sound, nodding her head in acknowledgment of the bear, a gesture that felt like a salutation. Andean emulated the nodding motion, hoping to communicate to her, *Hello, I am a friend.*

Taking in the rest of the cell, Andean noticed another cow asleep in the opposite corner. Peering further into the barn, she observed more cows confined in similar enclosures, their occasional groans echoing off the ceiling. Andean couldn't fathom such a life and pondered how these cows ended up in such dire circumstances.

Andean didn't know how much time she had spent by the barn that night but did not want to leave. She felt connected to them, especially the first cow she had met. The two spent a lot of time studying one another, observing their differences, physical and situational. Out of curiosity, Andean made some gestures with her head, shaking her head back and forth to make her ears flop, to see if the cow might respond. To her excitement, the cow shook her head, making her ears flop, too.

Andean's spirits soared as they exchanged playful movements, with the cow responding enthusiastically. Their antics even garnered a reaction from the neighboring cow, who grunted and snorted in response. Amused but aware of the need to rest for the upcoming day, Andean reluctantly departed the barn, vowing to return the following night.

Phillip

With his avatar standing in the doorway, Phillip hesitated to touch the controller, wary of accidentally retracing his steps into the previous tunnel. Summoning his courage, he took a slow, deep breath and cautiously guided his avatar forward, eyes scanning for a save point. Much like the previous catacomb area, however, all he found was another hallway stretching ahead.

He could see up ahead that this one curved to the right. A glow flickered from around the bend, as if illuminated by flames. Forgetting about the time and his middle-schoolers, he sat up in his chair, leaned forward, and started his avatar jogging down the hallway. Sure enough, he found the hallway was lit by torches mounted on the wall. The skulls appeared to snarl and sneer as he trotted past them, the light from the flames casting shadows creating illusions of movement around him.

As Jethro rounded the corner, he was relieved to find the hallway ended and there was a door made of steel, partially rusted, that was ajar. The room had no torch light, but moonlight was shining in, casting a blue-white light revealing the stone floor and walls inside.

Advancing his avatar, Phillip pushed the door fully open, revealing a room filled with cells akin to an ancient prison or dungeon. Each cell was secured by rusted iron gates and large padlocks. Phillip guided Jethro to inspect each cell as they progressed, noting symbols carved into the stone at the back of each one. "It's a puzzle," he mused to himself, his intuition urging him to keep moving for now and return later with more clues.

Eager to find a save spot before potentially losing access to this secret level, Phillip pressed on, deciding to explore past the cells. As they reached the other end of the room, another door loomed ahead. Jethro approached it, and Phillip's avatar began to push it open, anticipation coursing through him.

Upon opening the door, he heard a roaring sound that sounded like rushing water in the distance. The walls were made of stone, crumbling and damp, water seeping through some of the crevices. He could hear Jethro's footsteps crunching along as he proceeded down this new hallway. Streaks of moonlight lit up the floor and walls. Jethro looked up and saw the tunnel had several metal grates lined up on the ceiling all the way down the hallway, where he could faintly see what looked like a waterfall up ahead.

Perplexed, he continued and, as he got closer, the roaring of the water grew louder and louder. As he approached it, he saw that it wasn't a waterfall but rather a very large culvert pipe with water gushing out, hard and fast, into a large reservoir deep below, probably at least 100 feet. No way Jethro could survive that plunge, and it was a risk he was not willing to take given his circumstances.

Backing away from the ledge, Phillip had Jethro look all around him to see if there were any other doors he might have missed. Perplexed, he looked up and saw a very large grate and could see the night sky up above. His eyes struggled to focus. He rubbed his eyes then his whole face, and then shook his head vigorously to try and wake himself up. Desperate to make more progress, he jogged back to the cells for clues. There must be a way to open the gates; maybe a switch on the ground or a loose skeleton bone to use as a lever somewhere. He tried opening the eight individual cells, using various combinations of buttons in front of each, but to no avail. As he inspected the interior of the cells, he found each furnished with a rough wooden bench. The ceilings, walls, and floors had what looked like scratch marks, made by a clawed or taloned beast.

After spending an inordinate amount of time going back and forth between the cells and waterfall, he was officially stumped. And very tired.

3:57 a.m.

After an exhaustive search, Phillip found himself at an impasse, his fatigue weighing heavily upon him. With the time ticking past 4:00 a.m., he realized the need for rest. Reluctantly, he set down the controller, leaving the game running, and retired to bed, surrendering to the embrace of sleep. Yet even in slumber, his mind remained ensnared by the labyrinthine tunnels, haunted by visions of QueenOfHearts666's praying mantis and the endless catacombs he now found himself navigating, a prisoner of his own dreams. In his dream, it was he who was running through the catacombs, not his avatar.

Two hours later, after what felt like only twenty minutes of sleep, Phillip was abruptly pulled from his maze dream into reality by his alarm. He felt like a zombie, but a burst of adrenaline hit him when he remembered the game and quickly sat up to see if it was still on. It was. Relieved, he pushed himself through his morning routine with what little energy he had. He stopped at a gas station to get an energy drink and pre-made breakfast sandwich, which he devoured, dreading the day ahead of him.

As he drove into the middle-school parking lot, he talked himself through his lesson plan for the day. As he prepared for his second period class, he conceded that he was not capable of teaching today. Bill Nye would have to take over for him after all. He made some quick worksheets for them to work on after that; it was the bare minimum but would have to suffice. As tired as he was, he spent most of his day reflecting on *Kingdom of Beasts* and the puzzle of the catacombs; jotting down rough sketches of what he could remember of the symbols, turning them this and that direction to see if he could find any patterns. His three classes came and went and, when the final bell rang at 3:20 he practiced self-control and stayed to grade the worksheets and enter their grades into the system.

His day had started with only one desire: to be back in his bed, asleep. But by the time he finished his grading he found he had caught a second wind of excitement. Would Jethro still be waiting for him in the catacombs when he got home?

Cadillac

Once Cadillac had finished devouring the rabbit, the wolves gradually rose, stretching their limbs before retreating back into the alcove, though not entirely. One of them, with a pointed stare and a subtle nod, signaled for her to follow. Cadillac hesitated for a moment, assessing their demeanor, before cautiously advancing. With a watchful eye, the wolves led her out of the alcove into the depths of the woods, periodically glancing back to ensure she trailed behind. Keeping her head low, Cadillac followed their lead, matching their steady pace.

As they journeyed deeper into the forest, they arrived at a larger rock formation. Approaching it, Cadillac discerned a deep alcove, its entrance shrouded in darkness. Inside, she spotted several other wolves nestled together. Some were asleep, but the soft sound of approaching footsteps roused them from their slumber.

Cadillac's three travel companions stepped aside and looked back at the docile canine who stood frozen in place, unsure of what to do. The other wolves lowered their heads, looking up at the dog from their shoulders. She saw them sniffing in her direction, taking in the scent of this strange visitor. A large white wolf began to walk towards her, teeth bared and shackles rising on the back of his neck, muscles stiffening as he began licking his snout and whiskers. He pawed and scratched at the ground, keeping his eyes on Cadillac. She could sense his hostility and took a few steps back, but the large black and brown wolf who rescued her stepped forward to confront him.

With growls reverberating between them, the two wolves circled each other, their eyes locked in a tense standoff. Cadillac felt a shiver run down her spine at the palpable tension in the air. Yet, her two protectors positioned themselves closer to her, silently asserting their readiness to defend her if necessary. Inside the cave, other wolves added their low, steady growls to the confrontation.

Cadillac's large friend looked back at her and the others and motioned his head forward, and the other two that had been shielding Cadillac entered the cave and she followed suit. She looked curiously from side to side as she passed by the other wolves in the cave. Some were lying down, others stood up from their resting positions in acknowledgement of their presence. They led her to a spot towards the back left side of the cave where other female wolves were congregating with smaller, younger looking wolves. Feeling safe and protected, she laid down next to the other female wolves as they surrounded her on all sides.

As Cadillac's adrenaline subsided, she became acutely aware of the aches and pains in her body. As she relaxed, the welts from mosquito bites itched and ached, and the scratches from navigating through harsh brambles began to sting. Her paws were raw and sore, and she realized she must have injured her hip at some point—probably from slipping along the side of a large rocky embankment held together mostly by tree roots. She had nearly fallen more than once, catching herself awkwardly and aggravating her right hip.

Sensing Cadillac's discomfort, one of the female wolves nestled herself behind Cadillac. The warmth and pressure of the wolf's muscled body against hers eased her aching muscles. The wolf lay down with her back against Cadillac's, then lifted her head and stared at Cadillac until she, too, lowered her head. She felt the wolf's breathing grow slower and steadier, a relaxing cadence that, along with her heartbeat and body heat, lulled Cadillac into a deep, restorative sleep.

Cadillac awoke to the sound of the wolves stirring and the movement of the wolf behind her. They were all rousing, even though the sun was lowering behind the western tree line. Stretching and yawning, the wolves made their way out of the cave. As Cadillac followed suit, she noticed that her sleeping partner had a swollen belly, chest, and nipples—she had a litter of pups on the way!

The wolf stretched and yawned, then proceeded toward the front of the cave with the others. Cadillac stood but hung back, unsure if she was expected to follow. Looking back at her, several wolves nodded toward the cave entrance, an invitation to join them. Although she had no idea where they were going, she did not sense any danger as she joined them outside the cave's entrance and melted into the dimly lit landscape.

Once out of the cave, the wolves positioned themselves in a predetermined formation. They stood in place for a long while, their breath creating puffs of steam that lingered in the air. Cadillac was captivated by their silence and stillness. She could sense the noiseless conversation infusing the pack, their eyes speaking volumes without a sound. As one, they disappeared into the woods.

They started with an easy, jaunting pace that felt almost playful but soon broke away from their synchronized trotting. The wolves took turns stopping and sniffing the ground around them, then sprinting back towards the front of the group.

Weaving in and out and among one another, there was a rhythm to their movements, a primal choreography embedded in their DNA. Cadillac didn't know what to do, so she focused on staying mostly in the center of the pack, watching their fluid movements and deciphering her role in this dance. The pregnant wolf stayed closest to her, using her nose and ears and other gestures to help Cadillac learn the intricate movements of the pack. Three wolves stayed behind them, guarding the rear, dashing back up along the perimeter of the pack then falling back behind Cadillac again; like a geese formation during migration, the wolves navigated through the frosty forest, whooshing past trees and rocks as if they, too, were in flight.

She realized that as they traveled, they were all steadily increasing their momentum. Running along with these wolves, Cadillac felt a kinship with them: their subtle rhythm impressing upon her psyche, like being home, but to no home she had ever known. Their cadence and fluidity resonated within her soul and she instinctively understood: *this was hunting*. It felt like family. She felt the urge to hunt welling inside of her, and her senses heightened to a level she had never experienced before.

The large brown and gray wolf whom she had first met was leading the pack and she recognized him as the Alpha. He slowed his pace and lowered his head, his signal to the pack that he had spotted their prey. Cadillac smelled the herd of deer before she saw them. The scent was familiar from her walks in the woods with Roland.

Heads hanging low and panting, the wolves descended upon the clearing where the deer were grazing and quietly trotted around the perimeter of the field. Despite their light treading, the deer were aware of them, their ears twitching and eyes wide with terror as they realized they were being hunted. Cadillac saw the first deer bolt to the right, and the pack descended upon the herd. Sprinting around them in circles, the wolves sought out the weakest target.

The wolves looked like swallows circling in the sky, swooping, stopping, and changing direction, then quickly darting left and right towards their potential victim. Cadillac hung back, watching the wolves work. She shifted her weight around as she stood in place, then paced back and forth in excited observation. She memorized each movement, surprised to find that she was already anticipating the next. Surprising herself, she released a stifled whimper at her eagerness to join her wolf friends in their hunt, but her nerves got the best of her.

Finally, the Alpha made his first attack on a deer they had managed to steer away from the rest of the herd. Lunging at her leg, the deer fell under the mighty grip of his jaw around her flesh, his teeth penetrating her right femur. Her body flailed to the ground, and still on her side, she tried desperately to stand back up again. However, in less time than it took her to gasp for air, two other wolves had already descended upon her. They held her down, and the Alpha released her leg, ran around to her head, and, without hesitation, bit down hard on her throat, tugging and pulling until she fell limp.

The rest of the wolves descended upon her carcass and began to tear her open, ripping large chunks of her flesh and eating voraciously. Their mouths and chests were covered in blood. Cadillac desperately wanted some of the meat, her stomach growling and saliva dripping from her teeth, but she waited for a sign from them to join, an invitation. She knew she was a guest and didn't dare come between the wolves and their feasting.

When the wolves gradually dispersed and most had finished, the Alpha walked over to Cadillac, licking his snout, blood staining the brown and silvery coat of his chest. He motioned with his head back towards the remains of the deer. Timidly, she walked toward the deer as he and the other wolves stood aside. She bent down and took a bite of the remains, then began to ravenously pick at the carcass. She felt that same instinctive delight that she had felt when eating the rabbit.

Cadillac picked furiously at the bones to get the scraps of meat that remained. She didn't notice at first, but crows began to fly overhead, becoming aware of them only when they began to swoop down to pick at the bones with her. She was startled away from her feasting when the wolves began to howl. Calling up to the sky, they congregated in the middle of the field and sang together. She turned from the carrion to join them, the vibrations of their song resonating in her chest.

Cadillac had never felt so alive. She followed them as they began to assemble back into their formation and headed back towards the woods. She herself now had blood stains on her fur. Composing herself, and confident in her new position, she joined them, and they did not question it. They had accepted her into their pack.

Andean

Andean continued to forage and eat all morning in preparation for the coming winter, but her evenings were spent at the farm with her new cow friend. They spoke volumes to one another without making a sound, the cow's eyes like windows into Andean's own soul. She felt connected to her, through a shared understanding of loss, but there was something more to the cow's sorrow; a helplessness caused by her days dictated by humans. The bear needed to understand more about what these cows were going through, with their udders bulging, scarred and stretched, engorged with milk, but with no babies to suckle them.

One morning, when she awoke, Andean decided she would venture down to the farm to get a closer look at what was happening in the buildings below. Keeping low, she crawled with her belly dragging against the cool dewy morning grass. She could hear many cows lowing and quickened her pace, her stomach in knots. She feared what she was going to see, already suspecting it would be something horrific.

As she approached the building, she saw cows' heads sticking out from the sides of the aluminum building. They were chewing some kind of milled grain held in metal cages just outside the building. An abomination, her heart ached, seeing them so restrained whilst trying to eat. Fixated on their distress, she found her legs carrying her still closer and closer, focused only on the cows and oblivious to the presence of any humans. She saw a tractor nearby that was big enough to hide behind, and galloped towards it to take cover while she got a closer look.

Once nestled behind the tractor, she could see clearly into the building and the sight turned her stomach: cows lined up, row after row, necks bound with collars and chained to metal cages holding them in place. Some were standing while others lay on the cement floor, neck harnesses just loose enough to allow them to move their heads, but not enough for them to move about. There were piles of grain in front of the cows, some of them chewing the grain slowly and mechanically, eyes lifeless and staring blankly at the food in front of them, their minds lost inside themselves. Andean waited until she was sure there were no humans in sight, then slowly crept out from behind the tractor to see more.

As she got closer, Andean could start to see into the building: aisles of cows muddled into a sea of black and white and brown that seemed to go on and on and, beyond this building, was a second building. The high aluminum ceilings reverberated overhead with the sound of their weak cries, mooing and whimpering. The harsh fluorescent lights hummed from the tin roofing and the animals had only cold hard cement to lay upon; no soft grass, no mossy dirt to cushion them, no sunlight to bathe in. They were all marked with yellow tags hanging from their ears.

Andean stood pondering, realizing she was holding her breath as she stayed deep in thought, wondering where their babies could be. A cold, damp breeze snapped her back into reality, reminding her that winter was looming, and she should be foraging. She left the farm that day completely changed; she felt anger and rage and compassion and sadness all at the same time. They shared the same grief of having their motherhoods stripped from them by humans.

Wandering the woods Andean decided to look for food to calm her mind. While she foraged, she considered what she had witnessed. She was provoked to do something, but was unsure of what, if anything, she could possibly do. She also could not continue along as though she had seen nothing. She wondered whether she could help some of them escape. She knew she couldn't save them all, but if she could at least free two or three it would be better than none.

Andean revisited a berry patch she had found a couple of days earlier and began to eat, her mind fixated on plans to free her friends. She would study the farm and the humans' routines. There was also the problem of the metal enclosure and tethering devices which would be impossible to claw or bite through. She had some experience trying to bend and lift metal; farm equipment left to rust in the woods made a good hiding spot for insects that she enjoyed munching on. On rare occasions during her trek westward, she found dumpsters filled with human trash including fresh food that was tossed aside and was quite adept at prying open metal cages filled with birdseed, her personal favorite treat.

But the metal structure and materials in this building looked far too thick and rigid even for her to mangle rough to release the cows.

After satiating herself with some roots and berries, she made her way back to her new nest and rested, her mind still swimming with the images of the cows trapped on that farm.

Maisie

Maisie was a Jersey cow who had only ever known life on a dairy farm. As a new calf, she had been pulled away from her mother within minutes of her birth. She remembered the moment vividly and it often haunted her dreams. She couldn't recall her mother's face, but her mother's cries stayed with her. Barely able to walk, she was dragged into a truck and driven to a place with harsh lights and strange men who poked and prodded her and then brought her to a large arena where she was auctioned off to a farmer who would be her owner.

The farmer kept her in a small pen along with many other baby cows, enclosed by chicken wire, with barely enough space for her to turn around. Maisie could hear the other young calves calling out, afraid and wanting their mothers. The first few nights she barely slept at all, overwhelmed by the strange noises and scents around her. She was cold and thirsty. She spent most of her time curled up in the back of her small white, plastic pen, sad and lonely, imagining life with a mother, and no fences.

Maisie's dreams were filled with the sadness of the day she was ripped away from her mother. She heard her mother's cries echoing around her in the darkness but could not find her. In these dreams, she would run from one end of the arena to the other, even circling the perimeter, but beyond the green metal fence was just empty bleachers, then blackness. Suspended from the center of the arena by a long chain was a dim light, which cast an eerie orange glow about her.

The bleachers were empty, but she could hear the crowd yelling out numbers and laughing, drowning out her empty cries. Her mother's bawling continued still through their raucous yelling and chatter, seemingly moving around the arena; every time she got close to it, she would suddenly hear it far away on the other side of the arena. Not even in her dreams could she escape the hell she woke up to every day.

The calves were fed regularly by strange humans who also cleaned up their feces and replenished their water. These humans moved silently and robotically from pen to pen until all the young cows were fed and their spaces cleaned. One day, Maisie saw some other cows being pulled by ropes from their pens and dragged into a large metal trailer that was hitched to a large black pickup truck. Gradually, the baby cows were taken one-by-one, led into the trailer and never seen again.

Eventually, it was Maisie's turn. Her heart raced with terror as she saw the farmers approaching her area. She cringed at the back of her pen, lying down and huddling as far back as she could. They noisily stepped in, ropes in hand, and tied one around her neck and snout. Maisie felt like she was suffocating. She planted her hooves firmly in the dirt, tugging against their pull, but they were too strong. She was dragged out of her pen, her legs weak from underuse.

The trailer loomed ahead, and Maisie began to feel dizzy. The humans talked to each other casually, unphased by her struggle.

"This one is feisty!" one laughed.

They pulled and pushed her until her legs gave out. Frightened and in pain, Maisie refused to stand, which only made them more aggressive. One of the humans retreated to the pickup truck and returned with a large yellow stick with metal prongs at the end.

Panting on the ground, Maisie watched helplessly as he approached with the ominous device. She tried to scramble to her feet, but she was too late. The man jabbed the prongs into her left hip, and Maisie was enveloped in a sharp, burning pain that radiated through her entire hindquarters, causing her to release her bladder. She bellowed in agony and bolted up, trying to run away, but her legs were weak and the pain from the shock lingered.

"There she goes," one said. "She'll learn soon."

She limped, defeated, up the ramp of the trailer where they hitched her near three other calves who had already been loaded and hitched as well. They did not make a sound but stared at her, horrified. Some had spittle hanging from their snouts and were breathing erratically. Looking into their eyes Maisie could feel their shared terror. The trailer was dark and silent but for the breathing of the forlorn animals. Musty, stained with manure and soaked with urine, the trailer reeked of fear. The truck lurched forward, yanking on the trailer which caused the young calves to stumble into one another, held upright only by the harnesses around their noses and mouths that attached them by chains to the trailer windows. Maisie felt nauseated.

The truck swerved and swayed as the wind whipped through the small, slotted windows of the trailer, stinging the calves' eyes with its harsh chill. Maisie began to shiver so fiercely that the muscles in her stomach and shoulders started to seize up. She couldn't tell if she was shivering from cold, fear, or both. Two of the other calves began calling out, bellowing over the sound of vehicles rushing past them on the interstate, terrified by the rushing scenery outside their windows. After what felt like an eternity, the truck slowed, making its way off the interstate and eventually to a new farm where Maisie would come to be held captive for many years.

During her first week on the farm, Maisie realized that resistance was futile. Noncompliance with orders was met with painful shoves and more prodding. She spent her days being led out to a pasture to graze, then brought back down to the barn and fed straw and grain. Days blended together, highlighted only by the time she could spend in the pasture with her barn mates. She found some comfort in bonding with the others during their time away from the humans. She noticed that a couple of her companions had swelling bellies and udders that were growing steadily.

One morning, over a year later, Maisie was brought to another building near the barn and, through an invasive and confusing procedure, was impregnated. Within a few months she could feel movement of the unborn calf inside of her and the memory of her own birth and separation from her mother came flooding back to her. It was comforting to feel her baby's movements inside her own body. For the first time in her life, she didn't feel lonely. Lying in her stall at night, she would reach to lick her belly, the pressure of her tongue pushing against the calf inside. The fluttery kicks of her calf's small hooves would sometimes send sharp pains through her pelvis and hips, but she welcomed them.

She had practiced numbing herself to the horrors she endured while living on the farm, but the pain of her pregnancy reminded her that she was, in fact, alive, and that there was a life inside of her, waiting to meet her.

As the months dragged on, Maisie's belly grew heavier. She was now being fed many times a day. She spent her days eating and lying down, then eating again, then lying down again. Time outside the barn was limited, but she looked forward to the fresh air whenever she could get it.

Maisie had always thought the worst day of her life was the day she was torn from her mother, but that paled in comparison to the day her first son was born. The sharp cramps came very early that morning, before sunrise, and she knew he was ready to meet her. Her breathing grew heavy, and she began pacing about, walking through the intense cramping she felt around her belly and pelvis.

A farmer had been checking on her regularly and, hearing her low moans and labored breathing, rushed off only to return quickly with two other men. She did not want them nearby, especially not touching her, but they insisted. They touched her almost constantly, distracting her from focusing on her son's birth, and only made the pain worse.

Finally, he was born. Maisie was exhausted, but upon seeing her little calf scrambling and crying on the ground, she quickly forgot about her pain and went to him, nuzzling and cleaning him off with her tongue. It was only for a few moments, though, as the men swiftly stole him away from her. At that moment, Maisie felt as if she had left her body. She watched in horror as he was dragged away, screaming in his weak newborn voice. This must be a nightmare, she thought.

But she couldn't wake up. She thrashed about trying to wake herself, hoping to find herself still pregnant, lying in her stall, but the gruesome reality continued. He eventually disappeared from view, but Maisie continued to lunge and bellow until she was physically spent and collapsed to the ground. She was reliving her trauma as a calf, ripped away from her mother violently, stuffed into a trailer, cold and scared, as if she had been born into hell, and knew he was in for a similar fate.

Over the years, Maisie birthed calf after calf on the dairy farm. Over time, she accepted the reality that they would be taken from her. Each time, she hoped the devastation of losing her calf would hurt less, but instead, it only compounded the sorrow she carried from all her losses. Maisie, and many other mothers, were hooked up to machines used to extract the milk from their udders for the farmers to sell.

For hours, they were milked, their udders swollen and sore, their feet tired from standing on the concrete of the milking area. The sensation of being milked only reminded them of the loss of their babies; the mechanical whirring and sucking sensation of the machines felt cold and lifeless against their teats.

Maisie's life became a joyless existence of mindless masticating, milking, sleeping, and more chewing and milking. Every day she woke up and wondered how many more days she would have to endure this tortured existence. Every day, that is, until the day she met the bear, staring at her from the window above her stall.

Phillip

Phillip emerged from the middle school building and walked briskly toward his car. He stared down at his phone with his headphones on to discourage his chatty colleagues from engaging him in tedious small talk. His mind was set on getting back to *Kingdom of Beasts*, worried that somehow the game might have restarted. He made it uninterrupted to his car, an old Honda Civic that always had some problem that needed fixing. Just as he got settled into his seat, his phone rang. It was his mother.

Annoyed, he closed the car door and braced himself for what he knew would be some kind of nagging conversation revolving around his social life, or lack thereof, or his career goals, which she seemed to find him devoid of entirely. It was as if she were projecting her dissatisfaction with her personal life choices onto him. The two of them had very different ideas about what success and happiness looked like, but the conflict was that she felt that only *her* definition of success was right, and he was just naive.

Phillip suspected that she secretly resented his gender identity and his transition from girl to boy and, while she affirmed acceptance of his identity (and his pronouns), he felt that

120

she silently blamed him for her ruined relationship with family who were "uncomfortable" with his transgender identity.

"They still see you as their niece and granddaughter is all," she would try to explain. "And now you look so…different; they have a hard time seeing past that, you know?"

Taking another deep breath, he answered his phone, bracing himself for her inevitable harangue on his dating life - her latest fixation.

"Hi, Mom."

"Don't sound so excited," she said, her typical response. "Excuse me for wanting to check in with you. Your father was asking me when you would be available to FaceTime and help him with his Bluetooth speakers. We can't seem to figure them out, and he keeps going on and on about these damn speakers. You know how he gets, all 'why don't they just make them like they used to' and carrying on."

He was half-listening as she went on and on about his father's impatience with technology. He rarely got a word in but made sure to throw in some 'Mmhmmms " and "Yups " so that she knew he was listening.

"Also, have you heard about all this business with those wolves up in New York?" I know you like all that science-animal stuff, but your dad and I saw on the news about how there have been sightings of wolves roaming around the woods of Upstate New York, which they said is very uncommon - I guess these wolves are endangered and mostly live up near Canada."

Phillip had heard about the wolf sightings, not just in New York but even some in southern Maine, and in Ohio. He had been keeping track of recent strange behavior being reported not only in wolves, but also in moose and bears as well. As an Earth Science teacher, and enthusiast, he had his theories on this strange behavior. Climate change has caused major impacts to the ecosystem and, as a result, on the migratory patterns and behaviors of all kinds of animals. Droughts, flooding, higher temperatures, all symptoms of climate change, were wreaking havoc on the animal habitats.

"Yes, I have been reading about that. I'm actually not surprised, based on historical shifts in the Earth's climate. There is correlation between the migratory patterns of…" he started but, not surprisingly, his mother interrupted:

"Oh, well, I didn't mean to get you started on one of your political rants, I just think it is scary; all these animals behaving strangely like that, and I worry that maybe it's a sign about some new super virus. You know how the animals can always sense these things before humans."

Phillip decided against debating with his obstinate mother, who often seemed to forget that he had earned degrees on the subject. Another disappointment to her was his career choice; she believed that teaching was more of a 'woman's job', which also confused him. Would she feel the same way had he not transitioned to a man? Of course not. She would have been proud of him if he had remained a 'she'.

His mind raced with the all too familiar thoughts and he felt a sudden urgency to get off the phone with her. She could get him so worked up but no matter how he responded, he was always being "too sensitive" or "too political", as if his gender identity had anything to do with politics.

"Mom, I've got to get going. I haven't left work yet and I need to get home to get some food."

If he told her he needed to get home because he wanted to play video games, he would have been forced to endure yet another lecture about how detrimental gaming was to his social life. But if he said he needed food, she returned to being the doting mother he remembered from his childhood.

"Yes, of course. You worry me, how thin you're getting. Are you getting enough sleep?"

She was stalling.

"Yes, plenty. But like I said, I've gotta go," he diverted.

"Okay, well, just let us know when you can help with the Bluetooth. How about we FaceTime Saturday?"

"Sure," he said as he turned on his ignition. "Okay, I'm about to start driving. I'll talk to you Saturday. Love you."

"Love you too," and before she could sneak in anything else, he hung up and stuffed his phone in his bag.

Phillip lived in Lakewood, a neighborhood in Long Beach. His roommate was probably at her girlfriend's house, since he noted her car missing when he pulled in next to her parking spot. He was relieved to be spared having to catch up with her; he barely saw Stephanie these days, but when she *was* home, she would want to catch him up on everything she had been doing and talk through her insecurities with her relationship with her girlfriend, Denisha. He snatched his bag from the passenger seat as he opened his door. It was a gorgeous L.A. day, hardly any clouds and a nice warm breeze.

His apartment was on the second floor of a three-story gated complex. He preferred to take the stairs, again, to avoid interacting with his neighbors. Most were very kind and eager for conversation, especially their neighbor next door who was always out walking his dog, a yellow lab named Bruce. Bruce seemed just as bored as Phillip when his owner, Carl, would stop to chat. Carl seemed to always have at least one or two rehearsed questions to pry Phillip with: was he having issues with his hot water, too? Had he tried the new Thai restaurant that opened two blocks down? Did he know anyone who could convert DVD's to digital? Phillip generally humored him, as he was not good at setting boundaries.

Luckily, there was no one mingling around the complex today. Phillip moved quickly, moving at a pace that he called "looking like you have to use the bathroom urgently," a universal language that should, if performed correctly, indicate to people nearby that they should not engage with you. He practically hopped up the last set of stairs and rounded the corner to his apartment. Opening the door, he popped his shoes off and immediately headed for his room.

Phillip's heart fluttered for a minute when he saw the screen was black but, as he grabbed for the controller he hit the analog button, and the screen came to life. Jethro the puma was still there, facing the waterfall, swaying in the place where he had left him. He sighed with relief and settled into his gaming chair. He spent a lot of time studying the wall, the waterfall, and the grate above him. Standing at the edge of the opening to the waterfall, he stared up at the night sky and studied the stars through the rusty iron grates. The game surprised him by zooming in at the night sky above him: there was something about the stars he was supposed to see. They must be part of the puzzle!

Phillip grabbed a piece of paper and drew the star patterns to see if there was some clue that might help him. Plotting the dots, he stared down at them. He pressed the 'back' button and was once again standing in at the edge of the ledge in front of the waterfall. He had Jethro retreat to the room with the cells, his paper with the star plots balancing on his right leg. Putting down the controller, he picked up his sketch and studied his star plot. Moving Jethro from cell to cell, he compared the dots he drew to the etchings on the cell walls. Phillip's stomach tightened as he came to one of the cells and found that, if connected just right, his dots matched the symbol on its back wall.

Again, Phillip put down his controller and began to look for his pencil, grabbing it from underneath his monitor, and slowly started connecting the dots on the paper, watching intently as each line he drew came together to recreate the symbol in front of him. As he connected the last dot, before he could even think about what it meant, the cell door swung open and the stone wall with the symbol on it started to shake, his controller rumbling in his lap, as the back wall slowly began to move back and to the right, revealing a dimly lit hallway.

Phillip sat in disbelief. He hadn't touched his controller! He retraced his movements in his mind: he had been drawing on the paper, the controller placed in his lap, so how did the game know he had discovered that the stars made up the same pattern as this symbol? Instinctively, he stood up and looked around him, feeling eerily like he was being watched. He wished Stephanie were home so she could be a witness to what had just happened.

Dumbfounded, and a bit creeped out, he considered shutting off the game, but instead tried to rationalize what had happened. Maybe his looking up at the stars and then standing in front of the correct cell was enough to advance him to the next screen. That must be it. The sequence he had followed, that's all. *I'm just being paranoid*, he finally reassured himself. There is no way the game could know that he plotted the stars on paper to solve the puzzle. Right?

Part II: The Initiation

Banks and Murders

Swans and crows are the wisest of the bird kingdom. That is, next to owls who, unlike swans and crows, are solitary creatures. Seeking the wisdom and sage advice of their owl sisters and brothers, swans and crows began to spread the prophetic messages of their owl brethren to all birds as they migrated across the globe: our Earth is in peril, change is coming, and we must prepare. After years of faithful observation, the owls and their moth followers had chosen those humans they deemed worthy to be recruited to assist in their survival of the Great Event.

Phillip Masterson was to be the first.

Sally

Sally had become obsessed with what she could only describe as 'the visitor.' Some creature had been in her hotel room and had tried to leave her a message, even if the message was just "hello." Usually, Sally would be afraid to imagine a stranger being in the hotel room with her, but there was something she couldn't pinpoint about this encounter that made her believe that this visitor was a friend and not dangerous.

After this last book signing event in Philadelphia there had been talks of a contract with a dog food company that wanted to mass produce some of April's biscuit recipes. Sally's face could potentially be on dog food packaging all over the country! A food label deal would also mean more traveling, more airplanes and more hotels. Sally was tired of the constant shuffling around from one place to the next. She already cringed whenever she saw April's assistant and had stopped caring when she heard the key card beeping behind the hotel door. The door would open, and Sally would barely even lift her head from the corner of the room in her bed. She would perk up her ears, certain that it was just April's assistant arriving on schedule to allow her a five-minute stroll in front of the hotel. If she was lucky, the hotel might have a small patch of grass where she could relieve herself, but often she would have to go so urgently that she couldn't make it to the grass and would pee right in the middle of the sidewalk, which always irritated the assistant.

"Seriously, Sally?!" he would exclaim, as if it were her fault that she had been stuck inside for too long with the pain of holding her bladder radiating up through her pelvis and into her chest.

Sally was now dedicating most of her time to sniffing around the hotel room, hoping to find the scent of the creature who had left her the mysterious food message. She was convinced that someone was trying to catch her attention and, starved for companionship, it was all she could think about. However, after three days in the hotel without any answers, Sally and April were on their way back to Manhattan.

Sally welcomed the familiarity of their apartment. She took in all the smells and sounds and enjoyed the comforts of her own things. Through the window, she watched the happenings on the street below: the garbage collectors tossing bags of trash into the back of their truck with little effort, the woman who walked to the same coffee shop at the same time every day, hair in a bonnet, sweatpants and slide-on sandals with socks, coming out with a coffee and white pastry bag, then back across the street to her apartment; the man with a black uniform and white apron smoking his cigarette while scrolling on his phone outside a local restaurant.

As the days passed, Sally began to gauge time using the schedules of pedestrians who walked by around the same time every day. She was able to recognize the humans who walked past around the same time that April would come home from her yoga class, or from her weekly meetings with her publicist, and correlated her arrivals and departures with the digital numbers on the microwave. Recently though, April's meetings had doubled in frequency, making it difficult for her to predict her comings and goings. With the pet food launch, April's time was consumed with endless video conferences and in-person meetings downtown.

Sally's IBS started to flare up again, but April wasn't walking her and instead entrusted her to the loathed assistant with the task, who was oblivious to her whimpers and caustic bowel movements. So, when she was scheduled for a photo shoot at a local restaurant, she grew increasingly anxious. It was a photo shoot for the debut of April's dog treat brand: *Tender Tasties*. The concept was for Sally to be in a high-end restaurant kitchen being served *Tender Tasties* on fancy plateware on the floor next to the counter, with the legs of a chef standing above her holding a treat as she looked up at him. Shortly into the photo shoot, though, Sally began to feel quite sick, her stomach cramped, and her mouth started sweating. She whimpered and tucked her tail between her legs, worried she was going to have an accident at any moment.

The photographer began to get frustrated with Sally, as he needed a shot of her looking up in anticipation for the treat, and one of her eating the treat. She refused to eat; the smell of the treat just made her stomach lurch, and she turned away from the "chef" model trying to offer her a sampling.

"Ugh, let's just reschedule. This isn't working," the photographer dramatically lamented.

April became frustrated with the photographer, which made Sally feel good. After arguing back and forth about rescheduling, April picked Sally up and left. As they left the building April held Sally close to her chest, aware of her physical discomfort, then brought her to a patch of grass. Sally had terrible diarrhea and April did her best to clean it up.

"I'm sorry sweetie," April said with sincerity. Sally began to feel better; April's concern was comforting.

"You want to go to the park?" she asked Sally.

Sally couldn't help but smile. Staring up at April she panted and wagged her tail, shaking her floppy ears lightly in appreciation of the gesture. April scooped her up again, gently, and held her until the Uber arrived to take them to the dog park.

Sally hadn't been able to play with other dogs for a long time and she was eager to make friends and enjoy the smells and sights of the park. It was one of her favorite dog parks, right near Central Park, and it had plenty of dirt for digging and space for sprinting around with other dogs. Sally loved seeing how fast she could go. She and her friends' favorite activity was running down the length of the park, and then doubling back to see who could go the fastest.

The Uber driver dropped them at the park and Sally's eyes lit up when she saw all the dogs there. April found a bench, unleashed Sally, and started tapping away at her phone. Sally ran out to greet the other dogs. After many excited introductions, and establishing boundaries with one another, as is customary with dogs, they started to play. She was a bit disappointed, however, to find that the dogs at the park today were engaged in a game of fetch with one of the owners. Sally did not like this fetching game; she found it redundant and boring. So, she entertained herself with her other favorite park activity: sniffing. Her keen nose could sniff out the smallest crumbs left by the humans snacking around the benches. She also enjoyed eating bugs and, so, spent some time hunting for ants and such to snack on.

Sally heard a chattering noise coming from above her and raised her head to see a brownish gray squirrel sitting on the fence staring down at her. She never trusted squirrels, as they seemed ready to attack her at any moment. They had an intensity in their eyes and movements that felt dangerous to her. She barked at the squirrel to try and scare him away, but the squirrel just sat still, barely flinching.

April yelled over to her to be quiet then resumed looking at her phone. Sally stopped barking and stared with curiosity at the squirrel. If she hadn't known any better, she would have thought the furry-tailed creature was smiling at her. She tilted her head, confused. The squirrel slowly descended the other side of the fence and, through the bars of the fence, started placing small sticks on the ground, crisscrossing them, as though he was building something. He looked up at Sally again, then back down at the sticks, then sniffed them and moved them about with her snout. She could see that this was some sort of message but could not decipher its meaning.

April glanced up and noticed that Sally was still sitting quietly in front of the fence and ran over, assuming that she was eating something harmful or disgusting. She grabbed Sally with rough hands and put her leash back on, promptly ending the park visit. April called another Uber and they were soon on their way back to the apartment.

Beatrice

Beatrice continued to journey to the hydrangea bush daily, where she and her animal friends watched videos together, hovering over the phone screen in wonder. As one video ended another one would soon follow and there they would stay, captivated, unaware of the passing of time. Beatrice and the others were baffled by human behavior: how they communicated, what motivated them, how they adorned themselves, how they reared their children, and, most terrifying, their violence and dysfunction.

Gradually and subtly, the animals were also learning to communicate with one other using their hands, arms, tails, feathers (if present) and assorted vocalizations. The swans often would honk felicitously at particularly jovial scenes involving animals. Their antics were quite infectious and often invoked the others to begin chittering along, sometimes causing Beatrice's stomach to contract and quiver. *Was this laughter?*

They learned about human tears, an expression that was often accompanied by dramatic, sweeping, sorrowful music. Sometimes humans would laugh and cry at the same time, their faces contorted in gruesome grimaces, red with tears flowing from their eyes, mucous streaming from their noses, some with spittle hanging from their mouths as they sobbed. Beatrice was confused by the intensity of their faces; it was as if they were in excruciating pain but had no visible injuries to speak of.

Beatrice had seen her fair share of gruesome accidents over the years, so it confused her to watch these humans carrying on as if in agony, but clearly uninjured. Even their own fellow humans, lying suffering on the streets and in physical pain, did not ignite in their faces the sadness she read in the visages behind the screen.

One day the racoon arrived in a panic, waving the phone frantically around the woodland gatherers shakily between both hands. They gathered around him and realized that it was no longer working. Beatrice's stomach sank. They all took turns poking and prodding it, but to no avail. Disappointment shadowed over the faces of the creatures gathered amongst the hydrangea roots.

Quite suddenly, one of the swans stepped forward, breaking the group from their trance of disbelief. He ruffled his feathers from neck to toe, as if shaking off the sadness that had descended upon the group. Composing himself, he summoned them to follow him out of their hydrangea hideout. Beatrice's heart pounded; watching him intently, her paws began to twitch with anticipation. She sensed his excitement and knew instinctively: he had a plan!

As they emerged from the foliage, they watched intently as he worked his way back towards the pond. He looked back at them for a moment and then, swiftly, took flight in the direction of a gathering of humans waiting in line to get tickets to ride the swan boats.

He landed next to the queue of people, and they began to point and smile. Many lifted their phones to take photos and videos of the spectacle. Beatrice was shocked when the swan swiftly hopped closer to them and, with his beak, knocked a phone out of one of the human's hands.

Alarmed, but still amused, the crowd began chattering, turning to one another and gesturing towards the swan. The human quickly stooped down in an attempt to retrieve the phone even as the swan was pecking at it, trying to grab it but unable to grip it in his smooth, flat beak. He began busking at the man: hissing, snorting, and flapping his wings to try and keep the human from the phone. Ultimately, the man kicked the swan away and grabbed his phone from the ground. The swan retreated, flying back in the direction of the group.

Just as quickly as he had joined them, he took off again in another direction, looking back over his shoulder as if to say, *follow me*. The swan took them even further away from the pond this time, to another part of the commons, where there were statues of ducks that tourists seemed to enjoy visiting. Beatrice realized she was the only one among them with the best chance of grabbing a phone once it fell to the ground. She was the fastest and had hands to grasp with.

When the swan maneuvered himself into the crowd of humans Beatrice bolted from underneath the tree where they had congregated. She kept her eyes on him the whole time, darting around legs, zigzagging her way through the crowd, the swan's feathers a blur as he moved among the people. When he zoomed in on his target, she bolted towards him.

Once again, he knocked a phone from one of their hands. Beatrice was right there and jumped atop it, but it was too heavy, and the human had recovered within seconds of the attack and was already reaching down to retrieve his phone. Beatrice darted away, discouraged. She hadn't thought about the weight of the phone. It was always the racoon who had carried their phone, with hands much larger and stronger than hers, but he couldn't move as quickly as the squirrel and his presence would be far too conspicuous.

Beatrice and the swan retreated again. As they worked their way back to the shade of a large oak tree, far from the humans, the swan tucked his feet under himself and assumed a resting position. The swan contemplated the group. All the conspirators (minus the turtle whom they had lost along the day's journey), understood the swan's intent, but were now aware of its flaw: the phones were too heavy for any of them to fetch faster than a human could retrieve it.

After some time, the swan took flight without warning, and the other two swans followed suit. They flew over the pond and away from the others. For a short while the rest of them just sat and stared at one another, unsure of what to do next. Gradually, one-by-one, they each began leaving the group, discouraged and forlorn.

Beatrice did not want to give up; she craved to learn more about what was motivating these humans and how they communicated to one another, and the phone had opened a portal to gain that knowledge.

Determined not to succumb to depression, she swiftly worked her way back to her drey, a nest she had constructed in a maple tree that she wedged between two smaller tree branches. Somehow, someway, she would get her hands on one of these phones.

Hunter

Hunter awoke, disoriented and nestled among large, knotted tree roots covered in pine needles. He had expected to be in his bed, as he had every morning since he could remember. But the reality of his escape and of his new surroundings hit him; the adrenaline of his realization caused him to stand up, alert, the fur along his back in raised hackles, anticipating some kind of danger but not being sure of what it could be. This was a new feeling; an awareness of being exposed and vulnerable; the survival instincts he never knew he had taken control.

Hunter's vision, his sense of smell, and particularly his hearing, all felt heightened. He was invigorated, at once overstimulated by all the newness of the sights, sounds, and odors around him, but simultaneously awestruck and excited. His awareness of the forest floor, moss, grass, and roots under his feet were sensations he had never experienced. Resentment rose in his gullet for the years he was bereft of the scents and noises of the world outside those house walls. Birds sang in the tree limbs above him in playful chirps and warbles, like a cherub choir welcoming the sun. It was the most beautiful orchestration he had ever heard.

The air was crisp and cool, and the fragrance of the damp pine needles, and moss overwhelmed his nostrils, their scent both pungent and sweet. Hunter faced the warmth of the sun and walked towards it graciously, still chilled from sleeping on the dank, cold ground. He was thirsty and recognized his need for water. He decided to walk close enough to the houses so that, should he change his mind about his escape, he could wander into somebody's yard who might be willing to take him in.

Hunter was sure he could hear the sound of rushing water. He followed his instincts and moved cautiously towards the swooshing, bubbling noise, treading slowly and slightly along toppled trees and mossy rocks. He stopped every ten feet or so to check the perimeter and listen for movement, glancing over each shoulder and sniffing to detect the scent of other animals. His nose was flooded with so many new smells, he wasn't sure which might be dangerous, and which were just the natural odors of the woods. The sound grew louder and sooner than he expected, and soon he found himself alongside a boisterous river with whitecaps toppling over large gray stones.

Hunter had never actually seen a river in real life but had spent a great deal of time watching the television with Faith and Henry, who always seemed to have the thing on, and he would see on the screen rivers and trees, forests, oceans, and many animal species. But experiencing it in real life felt surreal. Picking up his pace to a trot, he approached the shoreline and drank from the clear, crisp, fresh water. It was like nothing he had ever tasted! Icy cold and earthy, unlike the lukewarm, stagnant water that Faith would leave for him.

Hunter drank until his belly felt full, the frigid water reinvigorating him and completely quenching his thirst, another new sensation for him. He decided to continue his trek alongside the river, preferring to stay near it so that he could imbibe from it as needed. Hunter walked for a long time along the riverbank, startled every so often by camouflaged birds flying up from the ground in front of him as he approached; the sound of their flapping wings made him jump as they launched themselves up into the treetops above. He spotted chipmunks from time to time who scurried away when they saw him, ducking under leaves or inside of rotted tree trunks. His hunger pangs grew more intense, and he felt an instinctual desire to chase after the small critters. Not for entertainment, but as prey.

Hunter was familiar with mice while living with Faith and Henry. Aware of them, he recognized the sound of their scurrying in the walls at night, his urge to investigate causing him to leap from his bed and sniff along the floorboards. He had no desire to harm or kill them, but rather became curious about them; why were they in the house, what did they do during the day, and why did Faith want to kill them?

Hunter began to hear cars passing nearby as he continued along the riverbank. The woods were thinning out and his occasional sightings of buildings were becoming more frequent. The whooshing sound of cars grew louder, and he could see them just beyond the tree line to his left, traveling at speeds much faster than those in Henry and Faith's neighborhood. New smells began wafting from the city that he could see far in the distance, not as pleasant as those from the woods: warm and pungent, they smelled like an amalgamation of exhaust, festering trash, and heated pavement.

A loud rattling noise and sharp whistling sound sent him fleeing into some nearby brush. A train rushed by on the other side of the river, the rhythmic clanking filling his ears, causing him to flatten them against his head to protect them from the roaring noise. Even after the train had passed, he remained sheltered and tucked away in the brush while he composed himself.

As he rested there, he heard a cawing up above his head and looked up to see a big black crow staring down at him from a nearby pine tree. The crow seemed to be staring right back at him. Hunter waited for the crow to move. It did not. Hunter, curious about this strange behavior, maintained eye contact with the crow for quite some time. He stood staring up at it, transfixed, unable to look away and waiting in anticipation for…what? He was unsure, but waited, nonetheless.

The crow turned its head up toward the sky and began cawing rhythmically: caw, caw, caw, caw, four distinct caws in a row. Then, a few moments later, again: caw, caw, caw, caw. Again, just four cries followed by several seconds of silence. This was obviously not a song like the other birds he had heard; this felt different, like an announcement.

Hunter sat up from his crouched position in the brush, transfixed by the crow's presence and observed it attentively as it continued its steady cadence. Occasionally, between caws, it would spread its wings, flap and flutter them, then continued with its staccato cries. It was trying to get his attention; he was sure of it.

Then, as if reading his mind, it stopped and stared at Hunter with great intensity. Holding its gaze with him, the crow turned and bobbed its head up and down towards the city in the distance. Then, quite abruptly, it took flight from its perch in the pine tree, flying in the direction of the cityscape beyond the woods. Hunter turned and watched it as it soared overhead, gliding majestically over and across the river and landing among the branches of another coniferous tree just far enough away to appear silhouetted against the morning sky.

From afar Hunter could hear the crow calling out again in the same cadence: caw, caw, caw, caw. He felt compelled to follow, overwhelmed with a newfound sense of purpose. He began to pursue the crow along the river, walking briskly at first, unsure of his footing and still paranoid of unknown dangers, but soon found himself picking up his pace to a steady trot. His feet and legs began to feel more confident navigating among the rocks, ferns, and roots of the riverbank. The wind began to pick up, whipping across the water, blowing through his thick fur coat, and fueling his adrenaline.

He had never felt so alive.

Phillip

Phillip stood and stared at the entryway in front of him, his heart racing as he grasped for some scientific logic that might explain what had just occurred. He had definitely solved the code to open the secret door of the cell using paper and pencil. *But how did the game know?*

He debated whether to even continue, engrossed by the overwhelming feeling that by opening this hidden door, he was committing to something much bigger than a video game. He tried to fight this irrational premonition and, after much inner deliberation, decided the best path to conquering his fear was to forge ahead. A scientist at heart, he knew there had to be a reasonable explanation for this inexplicable phenomenon and was determined to solve the enigma.

Phillip steadied the controller in his hands and, taking a deep breath, guided his avatar through the doorway. He was still underground, but there were iron gates above him, moss and forest debris dangling down from between the slats. Moonlight filtered in, illuminating and revealing the dirt ground and walls around him, held in place by intricately woven tree roots. He could still hear rushing water all around him, as if he were traveling underground alongside a river. Water seeped through the walls, dripping down the mangled tree roots, and he was certain he could smell the damp moss and musty dirt walls around Jethro, even though it was just a game.

Almost instinctively, he began to slow Jethro's pace. Phillip sensed danger, expecting some foe to jump out in front of him. He took time to stop and take inventory of his stock of weapons and ammunition. He had been proud of the arsenal he had collected, managing to limit his use of ammunition by using his machete and claws for most of his battles. Phillip was able to increase his stamina and experience levels faster by limiting his use of long-range weapons, such as his shotgun or crossbow, and sticking to close-range combat weapons (machete, ax, or bludgeon). He found that guns were often not useful in situations where he felt Jethro was being hunted because his enemy could too easily predict his next move.

Phillip kept moving, wary of becoming a target, but kept his ax handy should he need to act quickly. One of Jethro's strengths, as a puma, was his speed and agility. He used this to his advantage, causing his enemies to waste their ammunition as they couldn't keep him in their crosshairs long enough to get a clean shot. Bullets flew around him and, at worst, only grazed him; nothing that his health tinctures (of which he had an abundance) couldn't remedy quickly during battle. Often, by the time they were able to get a shot off at him he was already pouncing on them with his mace or ax in hand.

Jethro continued down the tunnel, stopping every now and again in a defensive stance, ready for a jump scare and to fight. As he continued on, he finally saw ahead of him an opening at the end of the tunnel with a path leading up...and out. Jethro was now sprinting toward the exit. As he emerged from the underground, he could see before him a forest and, as he suspected, a river was flowing to his right. Pine trees towered over him, their heavy limbs swaying overhead.

Once out in the open, he was no longer controlling the progress as he realized it was the beginning of a cutscene. It was as if a drone was descending upon Jethro and he could see his puma from above, gusts of wind whipping so strongly that his short fur began to ripple. Jethro held his right arm and used his hand to shield his eyes from the strong gusts, his robe whipping wildly in the wind.

Panning back down to Jethro's field of sight, several shadowy figures began to emerge from the forest line in front of him. There was at least a dozen of them, all donned in red velvet hooded robes with tassels. They stepped towards him, each carrying a torch in their hands, like glowing bouquets of flowers, the flames dangerously close to their chests. Their faces were hidden behind the flames and the massive hoods hanging around their heads.

Phillip watched as the figures continued in a ceremonious pace towards him, one intentional step at a time, and slowly formed a semi-circle around him. He became aware of a dramatic rhythmic beat playing in the background that slowly crescendoed as the scene began to unfold. The drumbeats were soon accompanied by baritone chanting, presumably from the cloaked entourage surrounding Jethro.

The wind grew stronger as the chanting grew closer and louder. Pine needles fell like snow from above, swirling around the avatar as if caught in a cyclone. Standing on his hind legs, Jethro struggled to hold himself upright in the powerful gusts of wind whooshing up from the ground and around him. The robes and tassels of the figures flapped wildly but, despite the wind, their hoods remained draped over their heads and faces.

As the scene on his screen unfolded, Phillip realized that his own facial expression mirrored that of his avatar's; mouth ajar, speechless and confused, Jethro turned from side to side as he watched the hooded figures circle closer and closer, tightly surrounding him. He, like Jethro, found himself looking behind his shoulder, right to left, as if waiting for someone or something to come up behind him as well. But there was no one. His heart was racing and his palms were sweaty.

As the figures continued their dance around Jethro, a flapping sound, like reams of paper flying loose in the wind, began to accompany the chanting and rhythmic drumming. Flying over his avatar, a swarm of lunar moths and bats descended upon them. A tornado of winged night creatures flew around the perimeter of the group. The bats shrieked, their cries echoing against the trees.

The cutscene zoomed back down to Jethro's perspective, and Phillip found he had been holding his breath. Taking a deep breath, Phillip felt himself rejoined with his avatar in an unsettling out-of-body experience and quite abruptly found himself in control of his avatar again. The music and chanting stopped and the only sound he could hear was the rushing wind and flapping wings coming from the night creatures flying above him. The figures all stood still, the torches in their hands flickering violently in the wind but, somehow, staying alight despite the raging gusts.

Phillip held the controller (trying not to hold his breath) waiting for one of the other avatars to engage with him; his palms were sweaty, and he worried he might drop it. The figures, however, all remained motionless. Scanning the semi-circle before him, he observed their torches supported by large leather belts that they wore around their waists, like belts for carrying flagpoles. From underneath the long sleeves of the robes was revealed a diversity of paws, claws, and hooves holding the torches steady. Not knowing what else to do, he stepped forward.

As he approached them, each side of the semi-circled robed creatures repositioned themselves in an almost ghost-like, fluid movement, to form an aisle for him to walk through, facing one another and creating a path out towards the dark forest. The light from their torches was so bright that Phillip couldn't make out any details of the scene, only a dark silhouette of the tree line before him. Again, it was almost as if he himself could feel the heat of the torches warming his own cheeks as he led Jethro through their torch-lit path. Once he reached the end of their formation and left the bright flames behind, he could see the scene in front of him more clearly.

The trees were illuminated by moonlight, and Phillip saw standing before him a cloaked figure wearing a black (not red) robe, with large antlers protruding from its hood. Perched atop those antlers was a large brown and white speckled owl and several lunar moths, slowly pumping their luminous green and white wings that shimmered in the moonlight.

The figure raised his head and the avatar revealed itself as a large stag. The owl atop his antlers flapped his wings three times, causing the neighboring moths to momentarily flutter up and off the antlered branches before settling back down upon them. The stag's eyes were dark and intense and spoke volumes without a word. Phillip - no, Jethro - stared deep into those eyes, waiting for the stag to speak.

Phillip moved Jethro to step forward even closer, captivated by the scene unfolding before him. He could feel his heart beating in his ears as the stag, too, stepped forward. Phillip waited.

Then, not in the chat, but as dialogue in the game, the stag spoke:

"Welcome, Phillip."

Cadillac

Cadillac was now a member of the wolf pack, learning more and more every day about surviving without humans. It had been weeks since they had taken her in and she felt the air getting cooler and saw the leaves changing colors and falling, signs that winter was imminent. She learned that there were two pack leaders: a male and a female. From the animals' interactions she ascertained they were mostly all family, born from its leaders and their spawn, many waiting to find mates of their own from other packs.

Together with the wolves, Cadillac learned to hunt and to scavenge, to hide when necessary, and how to mark their territory with urine and feces so that other wolves and hunting animals knew to stay away. She also learned how to cover up their tracks to put off scavengers like foxes, eager to step in and steal their hard-earned food.

At night the pack lay together, keeping one another warm. Together they dug dens for the newly born pups, who were still unable to see or hear, and the adults took turns caring for them. The other female wolves could produce milk when needed to help supplement the mother and relieve her of her nursing duties. The males took turns protecting the mother and pups and brought them food.

The pack set out one evening for a hunt. The new pups were ready to start eating meat now that they needed more than just milk to keep them nourished. Cadillac was well-versed in her role in the hunt. After the Alpha pulled the beast to the ground, the Betas would come to restrain their prey, allowing the Alpha to make the final kill, and it was Cadillac's job to monitor the perimeter for potential predators lurking to attack the spoils. She would circle the kill site, and sniff and listen for danger. Once the Alphas stepped away, the Betas would take their turn eating and then, finally, she and the other Omega wolves would have their turn. As she and the others ate, the Alphas and Betas cleaned themselves and each other, licking blood from one another's jowls, necks, and paws.

When the hunters were satiated, Cadillac and the Omegas were to help bring meat back to the mothers and pups, holding a mouthful to bring back to the den. The youngest of the pups still needed the meat to be chewed for them. Some of the wolves would even regurgitate their food so the pups could eat and digest it more easily, as they needed to get used to the taste and new textures.

Cadillac was preparing to settle in for a nap with the pack, as was usual after a hunt, but as she circled around her sleeping area in the rear of the cave, the Alpha couple and two of the Beta wolves approached her. The female Alpha nodded her head at Cadillac, then motioned towards the forest behind them. They walked away and, without hesitation, she followed, excited and nervous at the same time to be summoned by the pack leaders. They moved at a deliberate pace, the wolves stopping occasionally to scan the treetops and perimeter, and to check for any dangerous scents.

It was eerily quiet. Cadillac, used to the comforting sounds of the pack moving around her, felt exposed and uneasy. The others, however, showed no signs of apprehension and walked with a calm cadence that she found reassuring. They stopped frequently, the Alphas scanning the treetops for something Cadillac could not see.

The silence was broken by a sharp cawing overhead. Four distinct caws, followed by silence. Then another four caws. The wolves stopped and, heads lifted to the sky, began to howl. Cadillac was startled but, as they howled, the female Alpha looked directly at her and held her gaze for several seconds. She was instructing her to 'howl.'

She began to howl as best she could, her vocal chords untrained to hit those tones. Timid at first, she soon let loose and howled with gusto up towards the sky. She was deeply moved by the reverberating notes that echoed among them and felt as if she herself was rooted to the earth below her: she was one with the earth below, above, and around her.

The male Alpha stopped howling and bowed his head and stretched his front legs out in front of him, putting his tail and rump in the air. Instinctively, the other wolves, and Cadillac, followed suit. Her heart was racing as she participated in this great ritual. Her ribs and chest fluttered, the air around her feeling electrical and causing her to shiver. Maintaining her bowed posture, she felt at once vulnerable and safe.

From the treetops came a loud flapping sound as a swarm of shadows swooped down around them. Cadillac looked up with her eyes, her head still bowed, and saw a murder of crows descending on them. The crows hovered down to the field just outside the tree line where the wolves had stopped, landing gracefully in front of them.

The crows began cawing in unison, some flapping their wings as they did so. Their caws echoed in and around the trees, creating an auditory illusion that they were surrounded completely by crows. Cadillac shivered and her eyes filled with wonder. One by one, the crows began to quiet until there was only one crow still cawing. It stood for a moment in front of the pack, then finished with one last set of caws: caw, caw, caw, caw.

The Alphas rose, prompting the rest of the pack to rise to their feet, as well. They arranged themselves to face the murder. The moon was so bright it reflected off their smooth, jet-black feathers, creating a blue iridescent glow around them. The Alphas licked their snouts and began to make hissing sneezing noises through their noses, shaking their heads as they did so. A crow from the front of the flock bobbed forward, bowing its head, extending its wings out, and rustling the feathers around its shoulders.

Standing upright again, the crow now turned its head towards the west. The Alphas turned to follow its gaze. The mountains in the distance already had snow on their peaks which glistened bright white in the moonlight. As Cadillac stared out towards the westerly mountains, she saw a glimmer of light; it was as if the moonlight was reflecting off a piece of metal that was trembling in the wind.

The Alphas stepped back and turned to face the entire murder as their leader retreated among the flock. Without warning and to Cadillac's surprise, they took flight in unison, moving upward in a spiral; up above the Earth they flew, three times around like a tornado. They moved up and around, up and around again, then up once more, and finally flew west towards the glimmering light in the mountains.

The wolves and the dog watched in silence and stillness until the murder was nothing more than a dark cloud moving across the night sky. They stood together, captivated, until the Alphas finally turned to face them.

Giving the pack a subtle nod, they turned towards the forest ahead of them, running in the opposite direction as home.

Beatrice

Beatrice was now spending the largest part of her days looking for another phone. She had become obsessed with the device and the knowledge she was gaining from it. She barely ate, her mind had become so consumed with human behavior that she was neglecting her own basic needs. She knew it would only be a matter of time before some careless human dropped one.

The young ones were especially oblivious, often distracted in conversation or roughhousing one another playfully, they didn't even notice as items fell to the ground from their backpacks. With each jovial step, their large packs would bounce upon their backs, the motion causing items to dislodge from its side pockets. Beatrice listened intently for the loud clacking noise of a phone falling against the hard sidewalk.

It had never occurred to the squirrel to retrieve a phone before, as her primary interest had been the sugary or salty trails of food left behind by pedestrians as they walked. Sure, she was an expert at tracking food sources and finding the best neighborhoods for scavenging food; but scavenging for electronics was an entirely new endeavor, and the learning curve was consuming much of her time.

Beatrice felt a chill growing in the air. The days were growing shorter, and she knew she should be preparing for the winter ahead. Food would soon become scarce as fewer humans roamed the streets in the cold months and, even when they did, were not apt to sit outside on the benches in the parks where she could collect the bits of food brushed off their laps onto the ground.

From atop phone wires Beatrice intently watched the pedestrians below; up and down the streets they paced by, steps quick and intentional in the cold, brisk autumn weather. Many of them were already wearing gloves and mittens, leaving their phones in their jacket pockets where they were more likely to slip out and to the ground. These became her primary targets.

The weight of the phone itself was the other obstacle she needed to sort through. Even if one of the human cubs were to carelessly drop a phone, she would still need to use her mouth and hands to drag it away and out of sight, which could be conspicuous. Her plan was to haul it beneath nearby shrubbery or hide it under leaves or trash. Then, later, she could bring the other members of her clandestine team to the phone. She realized she might not be able to find them again, but she couldn't give up.

Then, one day, as she systematically monitored the sidewalk from atop some wires, she found it: a shiny black rectangle lying in some taller grass next to the sidewalk. Passersby did not take notice of it there, lying face down, its black case blending into the dark growth under the grass. Tail twitching, Beatrice quickly commenced her descent to the sidewalk below, fearful some good Samaritan might beat her to it.

She did not take her eyes off the phone for a moment as she darted down the telephone pole. Keeping her eyes locked on the ground below, she dug her claws deeper into the wooden pole as she began her descent to the sidewalk below. As soon as she made contact with the sidewalk below, she zig-zagged her way over to the patch of grass with the phone, barely dodging a French bulldog who lunged at her, its slobbering jowls coming within inches of Beatrice's throat. The beast was quickly pulled back by its owner, resulting in a deluge of spilled coffee followed by a tirade of foul language offensive even by Boston standards.

Beatrice threw herself upon the phone and, with her hands, pushed the device across the sidewalk, stopping to pull for a bit and then push again, fearful that at any moment a human would recognize her find and shoo her away. Fortunately, she spotted a paper bag in a heap of greasy crinkled food wrappers at the base of a nearby brick building.

She propped the phone against the wall for leverage and managed to shove it neatly into the bag. Beatrice grabbed the food wrappers and napkins and shoved them inside of the paper bag, pushing the phone to the bottom, then dragged it away to a nearby alley. There, under a dumpster, she tucked the paper bag away, rearranging more trash in front of it so that no one might be tempted to pick it up.

Beatrice spent quite a bit of time committing the nearby landmarks to her memory including the symbols and numbers printed on the dumpster that the humans used for identification. She had the uncanny ability to remember these kinds of symbols unlike any other squirrel she had known and had no doubt she could lead her friends back to this exact location.

Beatrice began her trek back to the Boston Common. Her heart pumped with the adrenaline caused by her discovery, and she was eager to share her excitement with her co-conspirators. Hopping from branch to branch, climbing up telephone poles and scurrying across wires far above the asphalt below, Beatrice lost track of time and distance. In her eagerness to get back to her friends, she felt as if she had been running for hours, but likely no more than twenty minutes had passed by the time she reached the Common.

Once at the Common, Beatrice stopped to scan the perimeter, hoping to see the flick of a fellow woodland creature's tail or flap of a white-feathered wing, signaling her to join them. There were no tails flicking to catch her attention but, as she had hoped, she caught sight of some white feathers flapping in the shrubbery across the way.

Without hesitation, she darted towards the rustling leaves and feathers, her heart racing with excitement, eager to share with them the news of her discovery. Beatrice scooted into the shrubs and practically leapt into the center of their small clearing among the hydrangeas, surprised to see many of her woodland friends already waiting for her in expectation. Catching her even more off guard were three crows perched in the branches above them, solemnly waiting along with her friends.

Once she had gathered her wits, Beatrice remembered her news and frantically dug around in the undergrowth, ripping up grass and shoving aside pebbles and dried hydrangea flowers and leaves to create a dirt patch in the center of the clearing. She snatched a small twig from a nearby limb and began etching the outline of a rectangle into the dirt on the ground before them.

As she worked, she looked up from time to time to assure she had their attention and observe the reactions in their eyes and body language. She began emulating the motions they used on the old phone on the dirt drawing beneath her: holding down a button, tapping on the screen with her full hand. They were captivated. She sat up, looking down at her drawing, then gazed among the critters and saw that they understood. They knew she had procured a phone.

One by one the others began to bob their heads in excitement. The swans lifted their heads to the roof and began honking and soon the crows joined them, cawing loudly towards the sky. The raccoon began flapping his ears and flicking his tail and the mice skirted in small circles around the webbed feet of the swans.

Once their excitement subsided, Beatrice flicked her tail four times, beckoning the others to follow, and bolted from the hideout.

Hunter

Hunter was now racing after the crow flying above him. When he stopped to catch his breath, the crow, too, would slow its pace, hovering down onto a nearby branch above, waiting to make sure the cat was still following him. Hunter had been so focused on following the crow that he hadn't had a chance to take in his new surroundings. Scanning the woods around him, he saw tall skyscrapers in the distance beyond the tree line. This was the city.

Hunter sat down, captivated by the scene of the city line before him. The crow began cawing again, which snapped him back into reality. He looked down at himself, paws covered in mud and mossy residue, fur matted in dirt with remnants of ferns and forest brush hanging from his orange and white coat. A compulsive groomer, Hunter was appalled. The crow, however, was obviously impatient, cawing and flapping its wings in his direction. So, as much as Hunter wanted desperately to clean himself, he knew he had to forge ahead.

The crow flew up from its perch, circled overhead and swooped in the direction of the cityscape. Hunter stood up and stretched, then began trotting below the tireless bird. He toggled his gaze from the crow above to the city ahead of him, amazed by its grandiosity. He found himself in a full gallop now, surprised by his athleticism as he navigated the uneven forest floor with its mossy rocks, pine needles, and precarious tree roots. Not once did he break his stride as his adrenaline was fueling his muscles. He powered forward, exhilarated, pushing himself to keep up with his avian friend above.

Hunter had no idea how long he had been running but somehow, he felt as if he could run forever, propelled by curiosity as to the crow's final destination. When the crow suddenly disappeared into the tops of the trees ahead of him, he slowed down from a sprint to a canter, and his muscles were screaming for him to rest. His pulse was throbbing in his toes, at the base of his whiskers, and the tips of his ears. His hunger pangs had disappeared, although he was unable to remember the last time he ate. But his throat, burning and parched, screamed for water. He began panting, now desperate for water, but was able to push aside his discomfort and continue in the direction of the crow's descent.

Regrouping himself, Hunter bounded ahead in a sprint. He navigated swiftly through the brush and tree roots beneath him; the pads of his paws were sore and tender, but he persisted, nonetheless. He kept his gaze locked on the trees where the crow had taken cover: a totem in the labyrinth of the forest around him. Finally, he reached the tree and, as he approached it, saw a group of rats formed in a semi-circle at its base, as if they had been anticipating his arrival.

Hunter stopped in his tracks and surveyed the scene before him. As he scanned the group, the crow he had been following slowly drifted down from the tree above in a circular flight that landed it in the center of the group of rats. The crow flapped its wings and cawed loudly. The rats, as if following orders, began screeching and flicking their long, pink and black tails, some even bowing their heads to Hunter, whose heart was racing as he watched the strange dance unfold.

Out of nowhere, the rats were joined by several small red-eyed, green snakes that had slithered in from the forest. They swirled and writhed at the crow's talons, creating the illusion that the ground beneath the crow was rippling like lake water on a windy day. Fixated on the eerie scene, Hunter continued forward, drawn hypnotically towards the crow and its entourage, completely unafraid of the snakes slithering around its talons. The cat, overcome by an overwhelming sense of reverence for the creature, instinctively and deliberately approached the crow and bowed before it.

With its chest and feathers puffed, the magnificent black bird tipped its head towards one rat in particular. The rat obediently stepped forward, bowed his head, and approached Hunter. As they touched noses, Hunter felt an amiability towards this rat that he had not experienced with anyone before, not even Faith and Henry. The rat, seeming to reciprocate this amicable trust, gestured behind him and three of his rat companions came forward, dragging a mouse towards him. It was already dead. They gently placed the body in front of Hunter, as an offering.

Hunter's hunger, so long suppressed, took over and he began to devour the mouse. The mouse was still warm, and Hunter paused as the realization came over him: he had never experienced eating warm food before. Faith and Henry had always fed him dry kibble, his veterinarian insisting that they put him on a special diet to "combat his sedentary lifestyle". He found this offensive, as he was being held captive inside the house with no friends to play with, for hours, against his will.

Hunter became lost in the rapture of eating his first wild meal, almost forgetting about the rats, snakes, and crow standing around him. He could feel their eyes on him as he ate. The warm flesh of the mouse was full of flavor, tangy and savory, as it made its way down his gullet and into his stomach. As if awakening from a trance, Hunter lifted his face, the blood and flesh yet hanging from the white fur around his mouth. He stood tall, newly reborn into this unlikely family.

Cadillac

Cadillac and the pack had been traveling for maybe two hours and had finally stopped to sleep. She was starting to worry that she wouldn't be able to keep up much longer when the Alphas began slowing their pace, finally stopping and laying down in the soft, pillowy snow. While the hunters gathered for warmth to sleep in a large huddle, the Betas took turns keeping watch while the others rested. As she lay among the others, her mind replayed the events of the evening: the crows, the howling, and the strange glimmering light on the mountainside. A harrowing sense of dread overcame her, but her fatigued limbs and muscles begged for sleep. She allowed her mind to slip into a deep sleep and had lucid dreams of walking through the wintery forest with Roland.

Cadillac was roused by the Alphas sometime before dawn. A steady snow had taken hold, dropping several inches on the traveling pack. Cadillac found it comforting, the soft weight of the snow adding a layer of warmth over their huddled furry bodies. As her eyes adjusted to the morning light, she saw standing behind the Alpha pair one of the Beta wolves; the black wolf that had been with them when they first rescued her. They stood over her, pawing at the ground and making short, wet, sneezing sounds from their noses. She understood that they needed her to come with them. She stretched, shook the snow from her fur that had accumulated overnight, and followed them as they trotted away.

She followed them to a nearby hillside where she discovered a large brown rabbit lying limp and lifeless in the snow. As she neared it, she found that the others had positioned themselves behind her, their tails slowly swaying low and steady down the backs of their knees, their breath creating small puffs of mist that ascended into the air like clouds. Staring deeply into her eyes, they implored her to eat. They had a look in their eyes that she had not seen before, causing her stomach to feel as if it were filled with stones. She sensed concern, as if they were about to embark on a journey and would be away from the pack for some time, unsure of their return.

Cadillac wasn't hungry, but knew they were not asking her to eat. They were telling her she must. She used her paw to hold down the still-warm carcass while she tore at its fur and flesh. Ripping upwards, in two swift yanking motions, she was able to reveal the meat of the rabbit and began to eat. Its tangy warmth aroused her senses as she stood in the cold gusting wind, snow whipping against her muzzle, and she was brought into a state of full wakefulness. Oblivious to her surroundings, lost in the ritual of the feed and feeling safe with her siblings watching over her, she ate until satiated.

Cadillac raised her gaze and the wolves each gave a subtle nod and, before she could return the cue, they were off; their footprints the first of the woodland dwellers to christen the freshly fallen snow. As they ran across the field and into the forest, Cadillac was aware that above her, crows were flying and circling in the treetops. Their caws echoed in the frigid morning air around them and she could feel its shrill sound reverberate in her chest cavity. It was chilling and magical at the same time. With a pounding heart she followed the trail of snow dust and the clouds of the wolves' breath ahead of her.

Awestruck, she took in the icy landscape around her. Caught up in the majesty of the winter land, Cadillac jarred when the wolves stopped abruptly in front of her. Though they didn't look back, she felt them summoning her to their side, and she obeyed. Before them on the fresh snow was the lifeless body of a fox, its fur a vibrant red-orange, the tip of its tail a puff of dingy white and black offset by the luminous snow surrounding it. Its fur gently rustled in the wind that whistled over it. Arranged in a circle around the body were various branches and leaves. Small tracks could be seen scattered around the outside of the forest debris, left intentionally as if to memorialize the fox.

Slowly, one at a time, the wolves began to walk clockwise around the circle and, instinctively, Cadillac joined them. They all held their heads low, below their shoulders in ritualistic solemnity. They did not look directly at the body of the fox but, rather, kept their eyes fixed on the feet in front of them as they moved in unison around the body. Keeping her head and eyes low in solidarity, Cadillac felt an overwhelming grief consume her; the same feelings she had experienced when she lost Roland came flooding back, filling her chest and throat with a tight heaviness so intense she had to remind herself to breathe.

The wolves slowed their pace until the foremost wolf stopped. As Cadillac turned to face the fox, the other three wolves took positions standing to the north, east, and west of the fox. She understood that her position would be facing south. One by one, the wolves began sitting down slowly and intentionally into the cold, powdery snow. Cadillac sat, waiting for something but unsure of what to expect. She soon became aware of the cawing of crows above. She raised her eyes and saw them slowly drift down over the circle. Their dark silhouettes were peppered by the snow falling around them, as if sent from the very stars themselves, to meet them down on the frozen earth below. Like a helix descending from heaven, three crows landed softly next to the fox.

The female Alpha approached the fox, and the crows hopped backward. With care and reverence, she held the fox down with her right paw. The wolf hesitated, as if overcome by sudden sadness, but only for a moment before pushing her weight into the body, jaw locked around its shoulder, then yanked upwards in one smooth motion, tearing it apart to reveal the meat inside. Somberly, she stepped back out of the circle, leaving the fox behind. The crows, silent, bowed and tucked their heads into the crook of their wings. The snow flurried silently over the scene. Slowly, the crows sauntered towards the fox, their wingtips dragging through the snow behind them, and began to feed upon it.

The female Alpha pawed at the ground to get the attention of the others, snorting through her nose and licking her snout. It was time to go, she was saying. They continued in the same direction they had been traveling, none of them looking back. Picking up their pace, they ran along the forest floor, clumps of snow falling around them from the blanketed limbs of the pine trees above, sending bursts of snow clouds up from the ground into their faces.

The Alphas led the way, weaving back and forth as they ran, taking turns in the lead as Cadillac and the black Beta wolf hung back. With excitement, Cadillac realized that she and the Beta were beginning to weave in and around each other like the Alphas in front of them. She felt butterflies in her stomach, participating in this ritualistic dance with him: like geese in flight or swallows dancing in the sky, they were moving as one as they bounded through the thick snow underfoot. She lost awareness of her surroundings once again, her mind wandering back to the experience in the glade: an offering of a fox lay before them, but none partook. Instead, it was gifted to the crows. Even she, with her new taste for fresh, warm meat, had no desire to eat the fox when she saw it. This was different from a hunt. What she experienced was bigger than herself. She felt connected to the red critter herself, like… family.

Cadillac worked through her complicated feelings as she pushed through the snow with the pack leaders. She had disassociated herself from the feeling of her legs moving or of the air moving in and out of her lungs, or even the cold snow between her toes and burning sensation in her thighs. When the pack came to a sudden stop, she snapped back into the reality of the snowy forest around her. She shifted her focus forward to the wintry backdrop beyond their heads and shoulders. She found herself holding her breath, not knowing why. It was so quiet she could hear the snowflakes landing on the ground, a light sifting noise, like sand falling in a sand timer. The air was cold and damp; its moisture soothed her exhausted lungs.

As if out of thin air, she saw standing suddenly before them a large stag. He stood stock-still; if it weren't for the clouds of his breath that swirled in and around his large antlers Cadillac would have thought him a statue. She had never seen a stag before in her life. She was taken aback when the stag bowed his head and lowered himself, front legs down first, followed by his back legs, to the ground. Head still lowered, he remained motionless as Alphas lunged forward, the female clenching his neck with her jaws and pinning him down as the others descended upon him and, one quick movement ripped his jugular, rendering him lifeless within seconds.

Cadillac stood paralyzed. She was having an out-of-body experience, watching herself watch the others walking into the forest and gathering sticks and other tree debris. They placed their forest scraps in a circle around the stag's now lifeless body. She sensed they were not going to feed on him, either. He was to be another offering. Moving quickly, they soon had created a circle of sticks and stones around him; a shrine like that of the fox.

As they finished the circle, the wolves stepped back, turned towards her, and held her gaze intently. Their eyes were solemn and intense. Hers began to well with tears. She dared not look away, but wanted desperately for them to look away. Finally, as if one flesh, they all turned away from one another and the group bolted away in unison, continuing their journey southward.

Cadillac continued alongside them, again not looking back. She was beginning to understand.

Phillip

Phillip stood holding his controller, frozen in space. The game knew his name! His brain searched for logic, trying to make sense of what he had just heard and read on the screen in front of him.

"Welcome, Phillip."

That is what the stag had said: not his avatar's name, *his* actual name! Jethro stood before the stag; the cutscene had ended and the two were staring at one another. The stag was waiting for the puma to make the next move so, with the controller between his sweaty and unsteady hands, Phillip advanced Jethro towards the stag. His heart was in his throat as he approached the stag, and he was given the option to engage.

Press X to speak, he was prompted.

He pressed X and was given new options:

Y: *Hello, Gideon, I have traveled far and am glad to finally meet you.*

B: *I am sorry, I am lost and am not sure why I am here. Who are you?*

A: Please, I need to return to my kingdom. Can you help me get back?

X: *Send me home, now. I am betrayed.*

Phillip surveyed his bedroom, looking left, then right, then again over his shoulders, turning around sure he was being watched. He set down his controller on the dresser and reached for his phone. He opened his text messages and debated whether to text Stephanie about the bizarre, unsettling occurrence. He realized he didn't even know where to begin with an explanation. Still standing, in fact practically glued to the floor, he stared at his screen for several minutes. Finally, re-engaging with the game, he noted that Gideon the stag was waiting motionless, surrounded by the other hooded figures, while lunar moths continued to flutter and land on his antlers. The owl remained perched stoically upon him.

Phillip slowly lowered his phone to the dresser next to his TV, retrieving his controller again. What could he say to Stephanie, anyway? Hey, I think my game has become self-aware? He wished he had been able to take a screenshot of the stag speaking his name, but it was gone. Now he stood before the TV with four options. The logical side of his brain told him to press "B". This, after all, was how he truly felt and knew it should be his response. He took up the controller once more and without thinking about it, his thumb instinctively pressed "Y". It wasn't a slip. It was truly the response he wanted to give.

"We are glad you could join us, Jethro," the stag responded.

Again, Phillip was prompted to respond:

Y: *I am ready for my first mission. What do you need me to do?"*

B: *I fear I don't know why I'm here. Please, where am I?*

He didn't know why he was there but for some reason Phillip didn't seem to care. He really wanted to keep playing. He tapped his phone screen to check the time.

5:23 PM

It was still early.

He pressed "Y".

As soon as Phillip hit the button the game entered another cutscene. With the camera angle panning out, the robed figures resumed their chanting, starting low and quiet but rapidly growing louder and louder, the drum beat quickening. The robed creatures formed a circle around Jethro, who looked over one shoulder, then the next, turning around and around to watch as their torches' flames grew taller and taller. The sparks flew up in the night sky and burned out upon their ascent. He heard the wings and saw the shadows of bats flapping above him, flying fast and in unison counterclockwise above the circle; they were soon joined by giant lunar moths and other winged night creatures.

They flew so fast that they created an illusion of a black hole in the sky above Jethro, as if a portal were opening up above the puma. The cutscene angle took Phillip's vantage point up above the swirling black mass looking down on Jethro. He saw his avatar's eyes grow wide, mouth hanging in awe as an illuminated figure floated down from the vortex of the black cloud above.

It was QueenofHearts666.

As if riding a cloud, the Mantis gently glided down, their wings flapping rapidly in a blur of green and white, landing softly on the ground in front of Jethro. Phillip admired their robe of white, embellished with gold embroidery at the hems, paisley-like geometrics sparkled white and gold as they slowly approached him.

"Welcome, Phillip," they spoke. "We hoped you would come." The voice was ethereal, feminine, not man, yet not woman. They were both, and neither. Their skin was luminescent: green and pearly, shining iridescently, as if glowing from the inside out. Phillip quickly searched for his phone to try and get a picture of his name on the screen but, by the time he found it and unlocked it, the cutscene had advanced and his name disappeared.

The robed figures began to get down on one knee, one at a time, around the circle until they were all kneeling, their heads bowed and torches lifted from their belts that they now held firmly to the ground beside them.

"We have brought you here to enlist your help. The Kingdom is in peril. While we use many languages, we all speak the same. There is a darkness taking over the land, one that we have battled for centuries without the race of man. But we have learned that without men, the fight is futile."

Phillip's avatar spoke, without being prompted by the controller:

"We have Phillip now," Jethro spoke. "We can teach him our ways and help him spread our message to his kind."

The characters were now talking about Phillip in the third person, and it was apparent that Jethro himself was aware of his human counterpart. Phillip felt a strange sensation course through him that he could only describe as an out-of-body experience as he watched the scene unfold. An electric pricking feeling rippled up his spine and the back of his neck, then down the back of his legs and to his toes, causing him to shiver.

"Phillip must go to the Cairdean Forest. There he will meet Ethos, leader of the Silver Wolves. He will start his journey with them."

Jethro nodded, bowing his head. The robed animals all stepped back as did QueenofHearts666, gesturing with a long arm and wing towards the forest behind him.

"Go, now. Take with you this pendant," the enormous insect instructed him. They held out a dark obsidian prism hanging from a piece of twine. Jethro lowered his head to allow them to tie the pendant around his neck.

"You may now know my name: I am Nearta. We have many allies to help you along the way. But we also have many enemies. Stay safe, friend."

Phillip was in control again. The animals all stood still, their torches flickered, and their robes whipped in the wind, but otherwise they remained motionless. The flying creatures had all dispersed, disappearing into the night as quickly as they appeared. Phillip guided Jethro towards Nearta but found that the game would not let him engage with them anymore. Jethro jogged in place, unable to pass through the invisible wall that stood between him and the group. Moving around the circle, he found that his only option was to go in the direction towards which Nearta had gestured.

As he moved away from the circle and into the forest, the light of the torches grew dimmer and dimmer. He adjusted his eyes to the star and moonlight, gradually able to see into the trees around him, which he assumed was the Cairdean Forest. Most of the tree trunks were dark and shadowy, casting creepy silhouettes all around him, except for some birch trees whose white bark reflected the light of the moon, manifesting wispy, angelic figures that danced against the dark, ominous pine trees around them.

Jethro jogged along the mossy knotted roots, easily hopping over fallen logs and other forest debris. Unable to discern a clear trail, Phillip guided his avatar deeper into the woods, weaponless for the time being. He lost track of time as he darted back and forth between the trees, occasionally pausing to admire the enormity of some of them; they were crawling with ivy, their trunks wider than he was tall. Phillip was lost in the game, unmindful of any responsibilities or of the time. He seemed to be limitless in his opportunities to wander around this new setting. Prior to discovering this secret kingdom, the game had always kept his avatar from roaming outside its invisible boundaries. This forest offered freedom: nothing was off limits.

7:14 PM

Eventually, Phillip remembered his mission: to find the Silver Wolves and Ethos, their leader. He was given no other information than to find them in the forest, but the forest seemed to go on and on. He hadn't seen any other animals and noticed that the sky in the distance was starting to get lighter; the stars gradually faded as the sunlight crept in from the east and the pine trees, which had been nothing but black shadows in the dark, were now revealed to show majestic large boughs with deep green foliage. He began to hear birds chirping in the trees around him.

Caught up in the game, he jumped when his phone started to ring and vibrate on the dresser in front of him. He set down his controller and grabbed his phone. It was his mother.

"Ugh," he said to himself, holding the phone in one hand and placing the controller gently on the dresser with the other. Keeping his eyes on Jethro, he answered.

"Hi Mom."

"Don't sound so excited," she said sarcastically. "Dad was hoping you could help him get his new Bluetooth speakers set up this weekend. Are you around so we can FaceTime?"

Phillip rolled his eyes. His father could be so infantile, and he didn't understand why his mother catered to his tantrums.

"Sure, yeah," he responded, eyes still glued to Jethro and the colorful landscape around him. As she talked at him, he took in the graphics of the game: the sunlight now revealed rich browns and greens of the forest floor, rotting tree trunks covered in mossy palettes of emerald, olive, and dark seaweed; a living carpet growing up and around the tree trunks, covering them like a blanket. He began to feel a tension in his stomach, all of a sudden realizing how exposed Jethro was, and pulled out his axe.

"Wonderful. How about you call us around 9:00? We are going to be running errands on Saturday, later in the morning. There is a plant sale downtown and I want to make sure I get there before all the good perennials are snatched up. You know you haven't come out to visit in a while. The gardens are coming along nicely."

"Mm-hmm," he responded, half-listening and half-planning which direction he would go next, his eyes scanning the area around him for signs of movement. He was looking for wolves. Ethos, was the leader's name. He started mumbling the name under his breath as his mother talked so he wouldn't forget.

"Anyways," she continued, "what have you been up to?"

"Oh…" he paused. "Not much. Working mostly."

He could tell his mother was irritated by his lack of engagement.

"Well, okay, I guess you have better things to do," she said.

Phillip rolled his eyes. His mother, the master of manipulation, always knew what to say to trigger his guilt for not being the daughter she had hoped for.

"Sorry Mom, I was in the middle of grading papers," he lied. He knew she would get upset if she knew he was playing video games. "I'm just a little distracted is all. But yes, I'll FaceTime you on Saturday. Um, how's Adam doing?" His best defense was to bring up one of his siblings when he could sense she was feeling neglected by him.

"Oh, he is doing alright. He's getting ready for midterms, I think. He has a girlfriend I guess, someone he met in one of his political science classes." Adam had plans to go to law school and their parents were pleased at his prospects, thinking mostly of his potential salary as a lawyer. They had always measured success by how much money someone made, managing to turn Phillip's passion for teaching into some kind of shortcoming. He imagined that if he hadn't transitioned, they would have been proud of "her" so long as "she" married someone more financially successful than "she".

Miraculously, his mother interrupted his thoughts.

"Oh, Phillip, I'm sorry sweetheart but someone is at the door, and I think it's the cable company. We needed to get one of those wi-fi extender things, so they are coming to help us set it up. We'll talk this weekend. Love you!"

He barely had time to say goodbye to her as she hung up abruptly. Relieved, he put his phone down and, taking his controller again in both hands, moved Jethro forward. The forest floor was now completely visible in the daylight. As the puma advanced towards the east, the rising sun shining directly on his face, a large black wolf came at him out of nowhere, pinning him to the ground.

The game once again went into a cutscene, with the wolf holding Jethro to the ground by his neck. Phillip could see blood being drawn around his avatar's neck and heard the wolf's low growl; its ears were back and flat against its head. As Jethro was held down, the scene panned out to reveal a pack of black and silver coated wolves emerging from behind the trees, all wearing deerskin cloaks tied about their broad shoulders with rope.

Phillip was holding his breath again. *Breathe*, he told himself.

The largest black wolf, as big as a dire wolf, walked towards Jethro, who was still pinned to the ground.

"Who dares enter our forest?" he said in a low, austere voice.

Jethro was looking up from the ground, his face pressed against a tree root, as the large black wolf approached him, his nose now only inches away from Jethro's.

Y: Please don't hurt me, I come in peace, a messenger from the Alliance.

B: I have come as an offering to you, sent by the Alliance. I accept my fate.

Just then, Phillip was startled by a loud thunk against the window, and he jumped, dropping the controller to the floor. As it fell on the ground, a button was triggered, and Phillip glanced up to see which button he inadvertently chose. The cutscene continued with the wolf staring not at Jethro, but towards Phillip through the screen.

"We accept you as an offering, Phillip," said the black wolf. "You must go to Stephanie now." The screen began to grow brighter and brighter, the wolf and Jethro dimming from view, becoming so intense that the characters became completely obscured. Holding his hand to shield his eyes, the TV screen's brightness crescendoed into a flash, causing Phillip to close his eyes.

When he opened them again, he saw Jethro standing once again in the hallway of the cells of the dark catacomb, facing an open cell door. From his position outside the cell, he could see another symbol on the wall opposite him, different from the one that had been there before.

Phillip felt like he was dreaming. Stephanie? He looked at his phone, saw the time was now 8:13, and anxiety grew in his stomach. He *must* be dreaming. *I need to wake up*, he told himself. *Wake up!* Recalling the loud noise that had startled him, he stretched and shook his head. He could feel his pulse throbbing in his neck and ears, reminding him that he was in fact awake, and alive. He slowly walked towards the window facing out to the front of the apartment building, not sure of what he would find but sure it was somehow related to the game.

Peering down below the windowsill from inside, he saw a starling lying by one of the chairs, its neck broken, and feathers disheveled. The outdoor lights cast an orange glow around it and, as Phillip looked closer, he saw that it held in its beak a purple and white pansy. *No way*, he thought. *Starlings aren't nocturnal. What is going on?*

Still feeling like he was in a trance, he became immobilized by the events unfolding around him and he stood lost in his thoughts, trying to make sense of his reality. His phone vibrated and rang in his hand, causing him to almost drop it. Stephanie was calling. His heart raced. *Had the game predicted her phone call?* His hand shook as he carefully pressed the green accept button.

"Hello?" he said, trying not to sound freaked out.

"Hey Phil!" Stephanie answered cheerfully. "Get your butt over here to Denisha's place. You said you were going to watch the *Misery* remake with us! You promised!"

"We miss you!" he heard Denisha yell in the background before he could respond. "No excuses," she continued. "I'm making enough tacos for four people, so you better not have me wasting this food!"

"Okay, I'm heading over now," he said without hesitation. "Rea…Really?" Stephanie sounded surprised, which was a valid reaction. He had been flaking out on them a lot lately and always found an excuse not to go over. "Okay! Great! That's so great! Oh, and can you pick up some drinks on the way?"

"Sure," he replied. "I'm on my way!"

Andean

Andean had built a den for herself not far from the farm. Every day she would wake up and lumber over to the hillside, sometimes seeing the cows grazing in the pasture but often wandering down to the barn to see her brown and white friend gazing at her through her barred window. Each day, Andean would walk a little closer to the cell. Often, they would just stare at the other, communicating with their eyes and subtle head tilts, the sorrow of their stares meeting somewhere in the space between them. They found comfort in one another's presence.

One day Andean realized she had spent the entire day watching her friend, who sometimes disappeared from the window, but she stayed near, not wanting to leave the cow all alone. On another day, when Andean woke up, she decided she would bring her friend some berries; a taste of something the cow wouldn't find in the fenced pastures.

Throughout her many visits, Andean had noted the schedules of the farmers who worked on the farm. She remembered at what point they would be out and about, working outside or in the cows' cells inside, depending on where the sun was in the sky. She knew when it would be safe for her to get down to the cow's cell without the risk of being seen. Her experience

187

with men was that when they saw bears or other wild creatures, they tried to capture or kill them.

Andean held the berries she had gathered in her paws as best she could, trying not to squeeze them too tightly as she slowly ambled towards the farm. She found she had to put her weight on her knuckles to preserve the berries held within her palm as she navigated through the woods. When she came to the fence, she gently laid the berries on the other side through the metal bars, hoisting herself up and down the other side, and then scooped the berries up again, along with some grass. She carefully moved down the pasture towards the barn below.

Andean approached the cow's cell, heard men's voices inside, and ducked into some shrubbery nearby to hide. Opening her paw, she saw that some of the berries had been crushed, their juice dripping down the side of her palm. She closed her paw around them once again, sat down and, using her other paw, held the berries up to her chest, like precious treasure, as she waited for the men to leave.

As she cradled the berries in her paw against her chest, she imagined holding her little Silver, protecting her precious cargo as if it were her child. The memory of the weight of his body against hers helped the time pass as she waited for the sun to move just above the barn, the time when the men would typically retreat to another location. Very slowly, she emerged from her hiding place, hand cramped around the berries and began crawling with just her back legs and left arm to brace her all the way down to her friend's cell.

Andean stayed low to the ground, focusing on each step intensely so as not to trip and fall, and found herself quite suddenly beneath the cow's window. Looking around her one last time, her ears alert and heart racing, she stood up and peered into the cell. The cow was lying on a pile of straw on the cement floor below. Andean, to get her attention, made some snorting noises through her nose that sounded very similar to a sneeze. The cow looked up, surprised, but not afraid. With some effort, she pushed herself up, first with her back legs, then with her front legs. Her udder hung low, worn and tattered.

She approached Andean, until their faces were within just a foot of one another through the bars. Carefully, Andean raised the berries up to the window, reaching her paw in as far as she could. Maisie reached through the bars with her tongue to taste the berries. She had never tasted anything so sweet in her life! Yet it was their tartness that reinvigorated her and left her wanting more.

The large bear watched in happiness as Maisie's eyes came to life, displaying a flicker of joy where once only despair lived. When the bear's paw had been licked clean, Andean reached again through the bars to touch the side of Maisie's face. They shared a common pain. The cow leaned her head into Andean, its weight against her paw familiar and comforting. It felt like trust. It felt like compassion. Andean could see Maisie's tail wagging. She felt that finally she had a purpose again, a reason to exist outside of just herself and, although she didn't want to leave, she knew the men would be returning soon.

Stroking Maisie's face one last time, Andean slowly pulled her hand from between the bars, backed up, and lowered herself to the ground. Maisie called out, already missing her friend. Andean motioned with her head in the direction of the men's voices, which were growing louder. Holding her paws to her face, she covered her eyes and wiped them off, then turned towards the woods again. Maisie, her eyes also filled with sadness, understood. But the despair soon melted away and hope filled her heart again: hope for something outside of the barn walls.

Andean awakened each morning to forage food for Maisie. Each time she descended the hillside she found Maisie waiting expectantly for her, ears perked, and shifting from side to side in excitement. On this particular day, she discovered some freshly fallen hickory nuts, crushing them with her jaws to reveal the meat inside. She mixed the meat of the nuts with some dandelion greens and, holding them in her paw, she ambled quickly along the pine needles on the forest floor, thrilled to share these new flavors with her friend.

As she approached Maisie's cell, Andean was alarmed to find she was not waiting at the window for her as she usually did. The big bear loped to the window and stood on her hind legs to peer in. There was a cow lying in the straw, but it was not Maisie. Devastated, she dropped the hickory nuts and dandelion greens to the ground. The unfamiliar cow inside merely glanced at her, then looked back down at the ground, uninterested in the bear outside her window.

Something bad had happened, Andean just knew it. She was overcome by a feeling of dread and sorrow, sure that she may never see her friend again.

Sam

Sam couldn't shake thoughts of the dog he had helped. Each morning, he woke up with a hopeful anticipation that he might find her wandering in the woods. Before their encounter, his days had blurred together into one long, monotonous haze, devoid of purpose; existing for the sake of existing. Now, a restless urge to search for something meaningful drove was motivating his daily activities.

The more he explored, the more he noticed peculiar signs: tree limbs laid upon the ground, placed in crosses or triangles, stones stacked atop one another for no apparent reason, sticks poked into the ground, all of it feeling very random yet intentional at the same time. Without understanding why, he, too, started grabbing sticks and stones and creating triangles and crosses, stacking stones on tree stumps, and moving pinecones around to form circles or diamonds on the forest floor. He felt compelled to leave his own message for the others: 'I understand', though he couldn't quite articulate what it was he understood.

When Sam counted stacks of stones five or seven stones high, he was compelled to try to see whether or not he could do better. So engrossed in his newfound task, Sam would sometimes forget to eat, his mind fully absorbed in creating these stone sculptures. It felt like a game, but he had no clue with whom he was playing or what the end goal was.

One day, feeling particularly playful, he ventured further from his den than ever before from his den. It had been a while since he found any new sculptures or patterns, and he suspected that whoever was leaving the stick and stone sculptures had moved on from the area. As he continued to search, he stumbled upon a neighborhood with houses and fenced-in yards. Anxious about interacting with humans, he decided to retreat towards the safety of the woods. He didn't get far though, and was stopped in his tracks when he saw, hanging from a nearby wooden fence, four tree limbs all dangling in a symmetric row, swaying lightly in the breeze.

There was a tree above the fence, so Sam expected that limbs and branches would naturally fall and get caught in fence beams from time to time. But this was different. The branches were spaced almost equally apart along the top of the fence, all around the same size, from one end of the fence to the other. It was obvious that they had been arranged there purposefully.

What creatures were responsible for this, he wondered. Sam felt the same urge he felt with stones creeping in; a compulsion to hang branches was compelling him. He began to walk towards the fence and, as he approached, he saw a man in sweatpants and an oversized sweater near another fence further down the way. He ducked low and back under the cover of a small pine tree nearby to observe the man. He watched in confusion as he saw the man taking sticks from the ground and arranging them on the fence, hanging them from one another to create a chain made of twigs.

The man stepped back to observe his work as the chain gently swayed in the breeze. When he turned, he spotted Sam. The little animal immediately froze, his stomach in a big knot, not sure if this man was trustworthy, but not afraid enough to run. Something in this man's eyes as he held his gaze told him he was friendly. Slowly, he sat back on his haunches. The man smiled, a warm and playful smile, like he was embarrassed to be caught in such a silly act; pleasantly surprised to find it was a groundhog and not another human. He laughed, said something unintelligible to Sam, waved, and moved on.

Sam watched the man as he walked away along the back of the fenced-in yards, hands in his pockets and humming a tune, looking up at the trees and birds, as if he had not one care in the world.

Luna

Luna was a rat who lived in a Hilton hotel in Philadelphia. She hadn't always lived in the hotel, but was currently stationed there, a member of the Alliance working to help spread the message to the dogs and cats tethered to their human owners: you are not alone! She and the other rats had already determined that the black boxes around the hotels were actually poisoned food, left as bait by the humans to kill them. They took notice when other rats would go into traps to eat and, not long after, they would become very sick and eventually die.

Humans seemed only interested in co-existing with very specific animals, under very specific conditions. This perplexed Luna and the other Alliance members. Word had spread of animals being imprisoned inside of large concrete buildings. The birds were able to observe some of their behavior from the tree limbs outside of the building windows and found it quite upsetting. Animals in cages, handled by humans in white jackets and wearing gloves and masks. They could sense fear in the animals' eyes. Something wasn't right.

Luna and the others spent their days watching humans come and go, paying attention to what they wore, what they carried, and the dogs that they walked with. Hiding in the shadows while the humans were distracted by their phones, the rats could slip easily into newly vacated rooms. There they would search for small objects to arrange in patterns to catch the attention of the dog staying there. Motivated by food, they were sure the dogs would notice the food having been tampered with.

It wasn't long before they revisited the rooms to find that the food was left untouched but was now arranged in a different pattern from the one the rats had left. The dogs had figured it out. Soon afterwards, the dogs began to create their own patterns with small objects left in the hotel hallways: they left candy wrappers or tissues outside of the doors that had other dogs inside, as they could easily smell one another, even through doors, to signal the rats that a message needed to be left for the dog inside.

Beatrice

Beatrice felt elated as she led the woodland critters out of their hiding space and back towards the alley where she had left the phone. She kept checking behind her to make sure she hadn't lost anyone, knowing she could be going twice as fast if it weren't for some of the others (the racoon was especially cumbersome, but also essential). One way or another, they all managed to track her, unscathed, through the Boston streets, most sprinting from shrub to shrub as Beatrice led the way from atop the phone wires and trees, while the swans flew above her, up and over the treetops.

Beatrice nearly slid past the alleyway, backtracking and causing some of the others to bump into one another. Skirting into the alley, she lunged under the dumpster and dragged the paper bag out using her teeth. She felt its weight and was relieved as she could tell the phone was still inside.

Opening the bag she rustled towards the bottom and dragged it out of the trash, presenting it to the rest of the group. She pushed it in front of the raccoon then backed away. The raccoon stared at the phone for just a few moments, still in disbelief of her heist, and then tapped on the glass screen. Numbers appeared on the screen and, moments later, disappeared. He tapped again and again. The numbers would appear, then disappear as the screen went black.

As Beatrice, the raccoon, possum, chipmunks, and mice hovered over the screen, the swans began to call up to the sky, flapping their wings as they did so. This startled the others at first but, looking up, they saw three crows hovering in circles above them, slowly descending upon the group. The group stood stunned as the crows landed softly among the array of critters. One crow stepped firmly forward and, using its beak, etched into some nearby dirt four numbers:

7344

Stepping back, it bobbed its head up and down in the direction of the phone. Beatrice understood. Using her tiny fingers, she tapped the screen to prompt the number pad, then entered the matching numbers. The screen illuminated and almost immediately vibrated and made a loud "ding", causing them all to step back in alarm.

On the screen a green box appeared with the symbols:

 Hello Beatrice!

Beatrice had learned her name.

Maisie

It was barely dawn when Maisie was awakened by the lights coming on in the barn, and the sound of men talking, their voices echoing between the stalls. Three men entered her stall holding ropes in their gloved hands. Backlit by the florescent lights above, their hats cast a malevolent shadow over their faces. She got to her feet shakily and slowly shuffled backwards towards the wall. Something wasn't right. Other cows began to stir and let out low moans that echoed across the metal ceiling.

Coming around her, the men quickly had her encircled and were able to attach a harness to her head and muzzle, despite her efforts to shake them away. The men spoke casually as they pulled her along, barely acknowledging her as they tugged her along behind them. A feeling of dread filled her chest, and her throat burned from the churning in her stomachs. As she emerged from the barn, she saw five other cows standing near a large truck with a ramp leading up to a barred trailer.

The men began pulling the cows up into the trailer. Maisie looked into the others' eyes and saw her own horror mirrored in their terrified gazes. This felt familiar. Like the day she was torn away from her mother.

The cows began to call out and wail as they slammed the back of the trailer shut. She heard the metallic jangle of a lock hitching outside, followed by two rhythmic pounding noises from a man outside, prompting the truck to lurch forward. They traveled at a great speed for what felt like an eternity until finally the truck came to a stop. Maisie's heart began to race. Her mouth was dry, and she was desperate for water.

Finally, they arrived at their destination. They had been driven to a large complex that had gates. The men stopped and talked with the guard, then were ushered through and continued until they reached a large industrial building. They heard a beeping noise as the truck began to move backwards then, suddenly, came to a stop, causing the cows to all lurch on their hooves. Her legs almost gave out under her as she heard them unlocking the door.

The gates swung open, and men began trudging up the ramp towards them. The cows all began to back up and away from them, screaming with terror, their eyes wide and their whites showing. Wearing leather gloves and work boots the men began unhitching the cows from the trailer and dragging them down the ramp. Maisie's hooves slipped against the metal, twisting her right knee on her descent. The men had long switches and were slapping them on the backs of their knees and thighs, even their stomachs, yelling and pushing them towards a large concrete building.

They were now being marched so close together Maisie's chin was forced up atop the rump of the cow in front of her, the tailbone of her fellow prisoner painfully hitting against her jaw as they were forced into a long concrete walkway. Once they were in the walkway, the men began removing their rope harnesses, and they had no way to go but forward, jammed together tightly between the concrete walls.

The screams of the cows were amplified as they echoed off the walls. Maisie began to feel dizzy, as she was being pushed forward by the panicked cows behind her, their hooves hitting against the back of her ankles, causing her to scream out.

Faintly ahead of her she began to hear popping sounds that grew louder as she was shoved along. The cries of the cows in front of her grew more panicked and soon the cows in front of her were trying to double back, some managing to scramble on top of others.

The popping went off rhythmically and each time Maisie felt the noise like a shock inside her skull. Finally, she spotted the source of the noise: several men were standing above the concrete walls with strange gun-like devices in their hands. She watched as one man touched the end of the device to the head of a cow in front of her. She couldn't see what had happened, but again heard the loud popping noise, then a thump.

Her vision started to get blurry, but she had no choice but to keep moving. She was now directly below the men but unable to straighten out her neck to see what they were doing.

Then, everything went black.

Phillip

Phillip grabbed his keys from the hook by the front door, nearly dropping them on the floor in his haste to get to Denisha's. Sliding on his favorite pair of crocs, he hesitated as he turned the doorknob. *Was this really happening?* He looked back into the apartment, scanning the living room and the adjoining areas. He wasn't even sure what he was looking for, but just felt a presence around him that he couldn't explain: something auspicious, not scary nor harmful, but a feeling in his bones telling him he needed to be with Stephanie and Denisha.

Phillip stepped out of his door, looking left then right down the apartment walkway; it was brown-painted concrete, spattered with bird droppings and crusted on seeds from the feeders he kept along the balcony railing. His landlord had complained, but Stephanie, understanding how important his birds were to Phillip, made sure to point out that there was nothing in the lease agreement preventing them from having bird feeders.

On the walkway below his bedroom window, he saw the starling still lying there, lifeless, the pansy still clasped in its beak. He bent down to examine it closer. As he did, a cold breeze came down from above him, causing the soft downy feathers around its shoulders to rustle. The pansy fluttered, reminding him of butterfly wings, then rolled out of its mouth and over to Phillip's feet. He picked it up and examined it.

Impulsively, he stood up and placed it gently in his pocket, then went back inside to retrieve a paper bag and rubber glove from underneath the sink. He put a glove on his right hand and bent down to pick up the bird, lifting it very gently from the concrete and slipping it into the paper bag. He folded the top of the bag over a couple of times and turned to lock the door behind him.

Phillip made his way down his apartment stairs, his senses heightened and alert, scanning for any fellow tenants who might want to engage with him so he could actively avoid them if necessary. He set down the paper bag as he got to the bottom of the stairs and put on the headphones that he had been wearing around his neck. He searched for an appropriately reverent place to leave the dead starling. It didn't feel right to just throw its body in the trash with fast food wrappers and bags of dog poop.

Just beyond the parking lot, he noticed a large tree sur-rounded by various perennial flowers planted along its trunk. Phillip walked towards the tree to find on closer inspection, a large meadow sage bush, whose purple blooms appeared to glow in the halogenic light of the streetlamp overhead.

Phillip carefully unfolded the paper bag and, very slowly, turned it upside down at the base of the bush. The star-ling rolled out gently, falling amongst the sage's lower foliage. Standing up, he reached into his pocket for his keys. As he did so, the pansy fell out, gliding angelically to the ground, landing near the starling. He left it there and was overcome by a heartfelt sadness in seeing the bird laid to rest with the sage. Solemnly, he turned away and headed towards his car.

Per Steph's request, he stopped on the way to get drinks at the grocery store and again he was overcome by the feeling of being watched; but not in a malicious way. He felt somehow comforted: a protective, invisible gaze. He didn't feel paranoid, just curious and even excited about the possibilities of what he had experienced that evening. Walking across the parking lot, he looked up and, unphased, noted a large brown owl perched atop one of the streetlamps staring down at him. He held its gaze, unflinching, for several seconds and, he was sure, saw the owl nod its head at him. He nodded back.

As Phillip resumed his walk towards the store, he shuffled past various debris, wrappers, cans, cups, and papers that he had become accustomed to as an L.A. pedestrian. There was always trash scattered about, but a particular array of litter in his path caught him off guard: three red solo plastic cups, each placed face down and in a triangle around a manhole cover. *Some bored college students thinking this was funny*, he pondered. Considering the events of the evening, however, he remained curiously suspicious.

As he neared the automatic doors of the store, his eye caught another pattern on the ground: someone had dropped some Goldfish crackers just outside the entrance, likely a distracted child, but what caused him to notice was that some of the fish had been arranged purposefully in neat a circle. He felt compelled to look back at the owl behind him, but it was no longer there.

Phillip grabbed a small grocery cart and navigated through the aisles to the drink section and picked up a couple of boxes of seltzers and some soda. His phone buzzed and he looked down and saw a text from Stephanie.

If it's not too late, can you grab a flank steak, too? Long story lol!

He swerved his cart in the opposite direction back towards the meat fridges and grabbed a flank steak. For some reason he held it in his hands for several seconds, feeling the cold meat through the plastic with his thumbs and thinking about the life it once lived. He didn't know why, but he felt suddenly sad.

Snapping back into reality, he worked his way back to the checkout, eager to leave and get to Denisha's. Back at the check-out, he set his items down on the conveyor belt, politely placing a yellow divider between his purchases and those of the person ahead of him. He pulled off his headphones and heard the cashier making small talk with the elderly man in front of him.

The cashier was a pleasant middle-aged woman, hair braided and secured atop her head, wearing large square framed glasses. She smiled at him and asked how his evening was going. They chatted while he put his card in the chip reader and plugged in his debit card pin. He met her eyes as she smiled and handed him the steak in one bag and the candy bar in another which he placed gently on top of the seltzer and soda in his cart.

"You have a good evening, now," she said.

"You as well," he replied. "Thank you."

Phillip pulled into Denisha's apartment complex about fifteen minutes later, parking in the visitor's lot. As he shifted his car into park, he sat for a few moments with butterflies in his stomach, not sure why he was so nervous. He grabbed his purchases and walked towards Denisha's unit. It was a bit of a juggling act to adjust the boxes of beverages he held between one arm and propped by his hip, but he managed to dig his phone out of his pocket and dial Steph as he approached the entrance to the building.

"Hey, I'm here," he said.

"Yay!" she exclaimed. "I'll buzz you in."

The door made the expected buzzing sound and then clicked open. He set the drinks on the counter to sign in with the front desk staff and headed to the third-floor apartment. Just as he knocked, the door opened, and Phillip was immediately greeted by Denisha who hugged him in spite of his encumbered arms.

"Here, let me grab those," she said as Stephanie playfully shuffled towards him, arms wide open waiting for a hug.

"We were sure you would bail! Come in, grab some food, and let's get this movie started. I'm so excited! This cast is fire, but I can't wait to see if they can compete with Kathy Bates' original performance."

Phillip was ushered into the kitchen where Denisha had tacos mostly assembled.

"Thanks for getting that steak," she said. "I thought we had some, which we do, but didn't realize we put it in the freezer."

"When she says 'we,' she is saying 'me'," clarified Stephanie.

"Let me cook up this steak real quick. You guys go ahead and start without me," said Denisha.

Phillip went into the living room and sat down on the couch and saw the movie was already queued up. He was quickly joined by their cat, Junie. She hopped up next to him, rubbing her face against his knee then jumped up on the back of the couch where she insisted on sniffing his beard and ears. The girls were still in the kitchen, being all cute together. Denisha stood by the stove caring for the steak while Stephanie grabbed a couple of seltzers, stopping to kiss Denisha and playfully pinch her butt before turning to join Phillip in the living room.

Stephanie came and plopped next to him, handing him a seltzer as she settled into her seat. Phillip noticed there was a laptop open on the coffee table in front of them. It was showing some kind of live feed of a laboratory. Denisha caught him leaning closer to look at the screen.

"Oh sorry," she called from the kitchen. "Yeah, they have me monitoring Caleb tonight. I have to keep it open and am supposed to jot down observations if I see him doing anything 'relevant,' but so far he's just been sleeping all evening."

Denisha was a lab technician working for a big tech company that was doing research on VR technology and its use in the medical field, something to do with neurology. She didn't talk much about it because she said she had signed a non-disclosure agreement and wasn't allowed to discuss her work. Phillip was sure they would frown upon her sharing this live feed with her friends but didn't say anything.

At one point, she confided in Stephanie and Phillip that her work involved VR chip implants that could be surgically implanted, allowing recipients to have a fully immersive gaming experience. She wouldn't give them more information than that, but Phillip was, of course, fascinated. Not that he imagined he would ever want to have such an implant himself. But he did wonder who *would* want such a thing, and how that would even work.

Stephanie started the movie, but Phillip was instantly distracted as he noticed movement in the live feed. Trying not to draw attention to himself, he looked up at the TV then back down at the laptop, watching curiously as Caleb, the chimpanzee, began to walk around his lab room. He had a bed, made with quilted blankets and even throw pillows, as well as a television set that was playing what looked like a wildlife documentary.

There were various toys around the lab room that looked like the toys you might see in a doctor's waiting room: colorful wooden beads that can be pushed along twisted metal like a roller-coaster, small bean bags with numbers and corresponding wooden boxes to put them in, a large rug with race car tracks printed on it. In addition to the race track rug was a large fuzzy emerald green rug in the center of the room with a table in the middle, atop which were puzzles and flashcards.

Phillip continued to look up at the movie then back down at the laptop. Stephanie was on IMDB letting him know about the cast and which actors had been in other movies they had seen. He was half-listening, but completely tuned her out when he saw Caleb start to crawl towards the table. He pulled himself upright to stand next to the table. He jumped when Caleb suddenly looked right at the camera, holding his gaze, and grabbing the pile of flashcards on top of the table.

Still maintaining eye contact with the camera, Caleb took the cards in his hand, moving to the far end of the table to completely face the camera, and then set them down in front of him. One at a time, he began to draw a card from the top of the pile and placed it, facedown, in front of him, followed by seven more cards, placed in a familiar pattern.

Denisha entered the living room holding platters of food, pushing the laptop over to make room for the spread.

"Here you go guys," she said. "Sorry about the wait. I'm gonna go grab some napkins and the sour cream."

"Hey, um, Denisha?" Phillip sat up and she turned around to look at him. "So, this may be perfectly normal, but is this something you would consider scientifically significant?" he asked, pointing to the laptop screen.

She walked over to the laptop and swung it around in her direction and pulled it close. Her eyes grew wide, and she stood to reach into her pocket to retrieve her phone and began texting furiously. Her phone vibrated and pinged almost immediately back.

"Hey guys, I'm so sorry, but I have to bail," she said, mostly looking at Stephanie with remorse in her eyes. "Yes, Phil, this is important. You guys go ahead and watch without me and eat! I've got to get to the lab."

Stephanie did not seem surprised, and mostly looked irritated, so Phillip gathered that this was a regular occurrence. Denisha, reading the disappointment in Steph's body language, sat next to her on the couch, placing her hand on the side of her face.

"I know, I know," Stephanie said, looking into Denisha's eyes as she held her face. "I understand, and I'm not mad but of course I'm upset. I know it's not your fault, it's your job. I get it."

Denisha gave her a kiss then headed to the bedroom and quickly returned wearing jeans and a t-shirt, pulling socks on her feet as she hopped her way to the front door. Junie leapt up off the couch and followed her, meowing at her as she walked away.

Phillip heard the clatter of keys and then heard her call out "Love you both, so sorry Phil! I hope we can try again soon!"

The door closed and Phillip felt the tension still lingering in the room.

"You okay?" he asked.

"I'll be okay," she said. "This has been happening a lot, is all. Some kind of 'breakthrough'. But of course, she can't talk about it."

She was quiet for a bit, so he got up to sit closer to her, letting her know she could talk more if she wanted.

"Ugh," she said, wiping away a tear. "Can we get out of here? I think I want to be at the apartment tonight. I don't know when she will be home. She rarely comes and stays with me anymore because she wants to be close to work."

"Sure," he said. "But I'm taking some of these tacos to go!" He smiled at her and she smiled back.

"Wanna play *Kingdom of Beasts* with me?" he asked.

"You know I'm not good at that game, but I'd love to half-watch you play and scroll through TikTok," she responded.

"You got it," he said.

Stephanie gathered her things and packed her bag quietly. He could feel her disappointment but did not attempt to fill the silence with small talk. That's what made their friendship so special: they respected one another's silence when working through complicated feelings.

"Hey," he said. "Do you want to just meet me back at the apartment? I'm happy to stay, too, but don't want you to feel rushed."

"Yeah, actually I do need to make sure Junie has food and grab some of my clothes out of the dryer."

"Cool. I'll see you soon," he said and gave her a hug.

Phillip stepped out of the apartment building into the cool night air, pulling his phone out of his pocket and began scrolling through his music playlists for the ride home.

Focused on the small screen, he was distracted by a loud bird call above him and, before he could pinpoint the source, a large bird swooped down and snatched the phone from his hands and flew off into the night.

Jered

Jered, a Swainson's Hawk, had been following Phillip for weeks now. He knew what his directive was but had to wait for the right opportunity. Lydia had told him that he would know when the moment presented itself. He was to look for the signs. So it was, on that night, he spotted Phillip below leaving the exact building where Lydia said he would find him. Diving off a branch from a nearby tree, he kept his sights on the phone in Phillip's hands, talons fully open and ready to snatch it. He knew he would only have one chance and that it was his impeccable aim that had landed him the mission. He had to calculate his trajectory without error.

The size and weight of the phone were concerning, and he had been practicing for weeks on the other humans holding their phones out in front of them. Jered found that the phones with plastic or rubber covers allowed him to dig his claws in long enough to maintain his grip. He hoped that Phillip's phone had such a case. His heart was in his throat and his eyes unblinking as his target grew closer and closer.

Jered swooped down, feet extended, as he pulled his wings back to slow his speed, claws open and locked on his target. Instinctively, and quite by accident, he let out a cry causing

Phillip to look up, but luckily, he looked up and behind him and did not see Jered approaching. Within feet of Phillip, he became flooded with adrenaline and surprised himself when he soon felt the phone in his grasp. He wasn't sure how he had even managed it, but he quickly flapped back upwards, determined to complete his mission.

His instinct was to clasp down around it quickly, as he would a small animal, but he remembered in his trials that this often caused the phone to pop out from his grip. So, with the phone cradled in his toes, he slowly curled his talons around the case. It was rubber. He was relieved. Now that he had it secured, he was still faced with the challenge of getting the phone to Lydia, who lived some distance away.

Jered's toes ached from the weight and width of the phone, stretching the limits of his feet. His wings flapped hard, pushing against the resistance of the phone cradled in his toes below him. He grew more and more concerned about dropping the phone, worried he might need to stop and find a place to safely land and resituate the phone in his claws. As he scanned the landscape below him, he felt a strong wind rush up from beneath him, pushing him forward and up in the direction of Lydia's apartment, providing much needed relief to his wings. He instinctively extended his wings without flapping, allowing the wind to magically carry him in the direction he needed to go.

Finally, he saw Lydia's high-rise apartment building. She lived in a top-floor penthouse suite and he could see her balcony in the distance, recognizable by all of the plants and shrubs she had planted up and around the balcony rails. As he started to descend to her balcony, he saw her there waiting for him. She wore a knee-length black pencil skirt and a white silk blouse, unbuttoned at the top, its fabric rippling in the wind. Her hair was pinned up and twisted around the top of her head, some strands hung loose and fluttered freely around her strong jawline.

When she saw Jered approach, she walked over to a padded lounge chair next to a gas fire pit filled with iridescent pebbles that glowed blue and orange in the flames. Circling down with the wind, using his wings as rudders against the current of the wind, he spiraled down to land clumsily beside her, the phone hitting the floor not more than five inches above the ground.

Lydia smiled and winked fondly at Jered, who stepped back and flapped his wings twice, basking in the pride he felt from her pleased face. Leaning down, ankles crossed and holding a champagne flute in her right hand, she collected Phillip's phone from the floor. Holding it proudly in her hand, she smiled and took a sip from her glass.

"Well done, Jered. We've found him, at last. We've found him."

She stood gracefully and began pacing slowly and intentionally, phone in hand, in her red-bottomed stiletto heels, traversing the marbled concrete patio with ease as she made her way to a stone water fountain adorned with cherub sculptures in the center. The stone cherubs were holding lambs and sitting, smiling playfully among potted rose bushes. She sat at last, this time at the edge of the stone fountain, crossing her legs and placing her glass with a gentle clink beside her.

Lydia opened the phone, relieved that the screen had not yet locked. She could have it unlocked, but this was so much more convenient. She opened the phone's settings and scrolled, screenshotted the information, then texted the screenshots to her own phone. Setting down Phillip's phone, she raised her own, reviewing the screenshots she had sent to herself.

She opened her contacts, scrolled a bit, then hovered over her contacts, bracing herself for the phone call she was about to make. This was really happening, after all these years of waiting. She clicked on the contact and began to ring. It barely rang once before they picked up.

"Do we have it?" came a voice immediately on the other end.

"Yes," said Lydia. "There is no going back now. Things are set in motion that cannot be undone."

"This was your idea," said the voice on the other end. "You said we could trust him. You'd better not let us down. For this to work, we need to know he can be trusted."

She felt pangs of guilt. She went rogue, but she couldn't just ignore her gut instincts. They were running out of time, and she figured it was easier to ask for forgiveness instead of permission. The animals had been letting her know they couldn't wait much longer, and she couldn't risk losing their trust.

"I appreciate your doubt," she said. "I would feel the same concern if I were in your position. Thank you for trusting me. You won't be disappointed, I promise."

"Don't make promises, especially well-intentioned ones," they responded. "Show me results, give me honesty, even when honesty doesn't always feel good to hear. Honesty is what is going to bring victory. Tell me your failures, don't hide them. Heroes don't hide their failures; they wear them like scars."

"I should have told you about Phillip before I set things in motion. I put both of us at risk when I did that. I am sorry," she confessed.

"Thank you. And I was too wrapped up in my ego to listen when you tried to present the idea to me. Things are moving faster than I would have liked, but we can't dwell on the past," the voice said, speaking to Lydia in a soothing, almost paternal tone, stern, but vulnerable.

"Okay, get some rest," they continued. "The Great Event is almost upon us. Don't do any more work tonight. Keep the phone safe. We will have plans in place to return it soon, but not until we can get it to Junox to do what he needs to do."

"I will," she lied, knowing she was far too excited to rest. She needed to go for a run.

Caleb

Caleb stood up from the table, stepping back and observing his work. This was sure to get his attention. He paced back and forth, admiring what he had done, an excitement taking over him. He could have run circles around the table. He wasn't sure how, but he knew the man from his dreams was watching him. The pattern that he had laid out with the cards had been haunting him.

In his dreams, he was looking up at the night sky and could see stars peeking out from the clouds in this unique arrangement. He obsessed over it daylong, grabbing rubber balls from his toy bins to try and recreate the pattern, placing them gently on the floor so that they did not roll out of formation. He didn't know what it meant but felt that it had some kind of meaning. Something important.

Quite suddenly he was overcome by the need to grab the flashcards and put them away, afraid that he was somehow revealing a secret, afraid the lab people would discover his creation. As best he could, he fumbled with them as he scooped them up from the table, returning them with the rest of the deck still in his hand, and placing them gently in the basket next to the table with the other testing materials.

There, he thought. *Maybe they won't notice.*

Caleb knew it was too late. He could feel he was now being watched by the bad people and the impulse to hide overcame him. Trembling, he started towards his bed in the corner, his legs and arms shaking as he made his way to the bed. He pulled back the white sheets and top blanket and slid underneath the covers. They felt cool and refreshing and he slid his feet back and forth against the smooth sheets for comfort. He pulled the blanket up and over his head, tugging at it to release it from under the mattress at the foot of the bed. He hated how tightly the lab staff tucked his bedding; it made him feel trapped, like when they would restrain him to perform their lab testing.

His heart began pounding faster and he tried to control his shaking breath under the covers. Caleb didn't know how he knew, but someone was about to come into his room. He could feel the moisture from his breath beginning to condense around his nose and mouth and curled himself up into a fetal position, trying to relax enough to stop shaking. Maybe if they thought he was asleep, they would leave him alone.

Beep. Click. Someone was entering the room.

"Hey Caleb," a soft voice announced. He recognized the voice. It was the kind woman with the gentle touch and soulful eyes. He liked her. He got the feeling that she didn't want to keep him in captivity.

He heard her approaching his bed and remained still, trying to control his breathing, hoping she would think him asleep, and leave. She sat down next to him. She could feel her weight behind him as he laid facing the wall, her presence comforting and found his breathing began to slow and his muscles relax.

"What were you doing up so late, playing with your cards?" she asked sincerely. He was afraid to acknowledge her, afraid of the impending wires and monitors and needles. He continued to lay still, holding himself in a fetal position whilst gripping his toes and feet with his hands, which were clammy from his anxiety.

"It's okay, Caleb," she finally said. "You've done nothing wrong."

She very slowly placed her hand on his shoulder over the covers and, when he didn't retreat from her touch, gently rubbed it. He began to cry, tears rolling down his cheeks and onto his pillow.

Why did it feel like he was in trouble? he asked himself.

He let the comfort of her warm touch linger on his shoulder, closing his eyes and wishing it would never end.

But, as he predicted, he heard the familiar beep and click sound of someone entering the room.

"When did you observe the behavior?" the male voice inquired.

Caleb winced, understanding every word that was being said. He was mad at himself for using the cards. He knew what would come from it – more tests and wires - and yet couldn't seem to stop himself.

"Roughly 2200 hours," she responded.

"This is significant. It means something. It must. Take screenshots of the footage and start running analyses to see if we can match the pattern with…something. Anything."

Caleb began to cry again, silently. Not even his own thoughts belonged to him anymore. He heard the sound of monitors being wheeled into his room. Another night without peace. He just wanted to be left alone. Or to be with the kind man from his dreams who taught him things. He wanted to sleep.

"Yes, sir," the woman answered, then shifted towards Caleb. "Alright, bud, I know you're tired, but we have to run some tests real quick, then you can rest. Okay?"

He didn't move but felt her gently rubbing his left shoulder. He could tell she also didn't want to do the tests.

"Great work," the man said. "I look forward to your report tomorrow."

Caleb heard the door click and felt her grip on his shoulder tighten as the steps outside the door grew fainter. He wanted to reach up and hold her hand but began to feel resentment knowing she would follow their orders.

"Okay Caleb, let's get this over with." Gently, she pulled the covers down from his head and gave him a soft kiss on the back of his head.

He wept silently while he waited and, as he lay with his eyes closed, felt for the first time felt hopeful. The man from his dreams would rescue him, he knew it.

Epilogue

Cadillac and Andean

Cadillac ran alongside Andean through the frigid Upstate New York forest. The air was quiet and still, the only sounds were an occasional cry from a crow in the distance and the crunching of their paws as they pushed through the twelve inches of ice-covered snow, weaving around trees and climbing over rotting logs, barely poking through the snow that laid over them like icing on a mossy cake. They were headed to their pasture to check on the progress of the digging around the metal fence.

As they approached the tree line just outside the pasture, they could see their woodland friends fast at work. Sam had recruited other groundhogs who, under the cover of the snow, were digging at the foundation of the posts below. Field mice and other smaller creatures, using their sharp claws and teeth, were working at the very base of the poles to crcatc an inch of space around the metal where the larger animals could not get to with their larger, clumsier paws. Andean and Cadillac had held their bladders all day, as the crew had encountered a set-back with the ground freezing, making it nearly impossible to dig through the ice.

Upon seeing Cadillac and Andean, Sam began chirping and sat up, whiskers and tail twitching, getting the attention of the others. Stopping their work, they saw their larger companions and moved away from the metal post. Andean and Cadillac took turns relieving themselves around the base of the metal, steam rising from the now wet ground below. They were mindful to not urinate over the snow enclave they had formed to keep the woodland creatures out of sight from predators and, most importantly, any of the men on the farm. They did not see much activity from the men during the winter, which was why they were spending their winter days battling the frozen ground.

After they had relieved themselves, the two then took turns pushing against the metal. They had already loosened the two posts around this one. They just needed to get them loose enough to be able to knock a section of the fence over large enough for the cows to get through come Spring. It wasn't moving as much as they had hoped. They would need more help.

As they continued shoving, arms and shoulders exhausted, several crows landed nearby to assess their progress. They could see more force would be needed. They flew up almost as quickly as they landed, off to find the stags, whose allegiance had finally been pledged after many years of opposition. Surely their strength coupled with their antlers could help move along the progress of the operation.

The smaller animals, seeing Cadillac and Andean stepping back to catch their breath and rest, stepped forward and began digging furiously again, taking advantage of the opportunity

226

to dig through the temporarily thawed ground. It was dirty work, but they kept in mind the end goal and pushed through their apprehension.

Cadillac motioned to Andean, sitting beside her, indicating they should go find more water to drink in the meantime. Andean wanted to stay and dig, desperate to see the fence section collapse. They chose a spot that Andean knew the men did not visit frequently, as far from the barn as possible. In this way, cows could slip through without being caught. Her concern was that all the cows would try to leave at once, instigating a search party by the men. She hoped that if they could release just one or two at a time, the broken fence wouldn't be mended until several had escaped. She knew they couldn't save them all. But it was better than doing nothing.

Andean, as she followed Cadillac, remembered the first day they met. Their friendship journey began a few days after Andean had realized that Maisie wasn't coming back. She fell again into a deep depression, full of fury and sadness that once again men had taken a loved one from her. She lay in her den all day, not able to eat, feeling sick with sorrow. She didn't know how much more her heart could take.

The urge to run away overcame her again, and she began wandering into the woods with no particular destination in mind. While walking, she heard loud barking and shrieking not far from her. They sounded like cries of sorrow, and she felt compelled to investigate. As she got closer, she could hear barking, almost shrill, and saw in the distance a house with large gardens outside. She ran towards the house and could see in the window a large dog scratching against the windows, desperate to escape. Overcome by the grief of Maisie's imprisonment and disappearance, she searched around the yard to find something to break into the house.

One of the garden beds had a large ornamental glass ball sitting upon a stone pedestal. She grabbed the ball with both front paws, centered herself under the weight of the ball, then pushed it up and away from her as hard as she could. It crashed into the window, glass shattering all over the porch below the window.

She became suddenly aware that she was outside of a human's home and became fearful of being discovered. But she had to make sure the dog had a way to escape whatever was happening inside. Composing herself, she bolted back into the woods and back to her den.

Andean never imagined she would see the dog again. Several weeks later, as she began hibernating, she was surprised to find the dog standing outside of her den, a freshly killed fish in her mouth which she dropped in front of Andean.

Coming soon: the second book of the Great Event Series, *Banks and Murders.*